Mamphela Ramphele

Women Changing the World

Aung San Suu Kyi
Standing Up for Democracy in Burma

Rigoberta Menchú
Defending Human Rights in Guatemala

Máiread Corrigan and Betty Williams
Making Peace in Northern Ireland

Mamphela Ramphele
Challenging Apartheid in South Africa

Ela Bhatt
Uniting Women in India

Advisory Board for Women Changing the World

Mamphela Ramphele

Challenging Apartheid in South Africa

Judith Harlan

The Feminist Press
at The City University of New York

Published by The Feminist Press at The City University of New York
The Graduate Center, 365 Fifth Avenue, New York, NY 10016

First edition, 2000

Library of Congress Cataloging-in-Publication Data

Harlan, Judith.
    Mamphela Ramphele: challenging apartheid in South Africa / by Judith Harlan.
      p.   cm. — (Women changing the world)
    Includes bibliographical references and index.
    Summary: A biography of Mamphela Ramphele, a woman who, as a medical doctor, teacher, anthropologist, and advisor to the Mandela government, challenged the racial and gender-based inequalities in South Africa.
    ISBN 1-55861-227-0 (alk. paper)—ISBN 1-55861-226-2 (pbk: alk. paper)
    1. Ramphele, Mamphela—Juvenile literature.   2. Women civil rights workers—South Africa—Biography—Juvenile literature.   3. Civil rights workers—South Africa—Biography—Juvenile literature. 4. Blacks—South Africa—Politics and government—Juvenile literature.   5. South Africa—Politics and government—1948–1994—Juvenile literature.   6. Women college administrators—South Africa— Biography—Juvenile literature.   7. College administrators—South Africa—Biography—Juvenile literature. [1. Ramphele, Mamphela.   2. Civil rights workers.   3. College administrators.   4. Blacks—South Africa.   5. Women—Biography.]
I. Title.   II. Series.

DT1949.R36 H37 2000+
305.42'092'26-dc21

99-039674
CIP

The Feminist Press is grateful to the Ford Foundation for their generous support of our work. The Feminist Press is also grateful to Mariam K. Chamberlain, Johnnetta B. Cole, Joanne Markell, Shirley Mow, Donna Schneier, and Genevieve Vaughan for their generosity in supporting this publication.

Text design by Dayna Navaro
Composition by CompuDesign, Charlottesville, Virginia
Printed on acid-free paper by RR Donnelley & Sons
Printed in Mexico

05   04   03   02   01   00   5   4   3   2   1

CONTENTS

Foreword

WHAT DOES IT TAKE TO CHANGE THE WORLD?

Maybe this question sounds overwhelming. However, people who become leaders have all had to ask themselves this question at some point. They started finding answers by choosing how they would lead their lives every day and by creating their own opportunities to make a difference in the world. The anthropologist Margaret Mead said, "Never doubt that a small group of thoughtful, committed citizens can change the world; indeed it's the only thing that ever has." So let's look at some of the qualities possessed by people who are determined to change the world.

First, it takes vision. The great stateswoman and humanitarian Eleanor Roosevelt said, "You must do the thing you think you cannot do." People who change the world have the ability to see what is wrong in their society. They also have the ability to imagine something new and better. They do not accept the way things *are*—the "status quo"— as the only way things *must be* or *can be*. It is this vision of an improved world that inspires others to join leaders in their efforts to make change. Leaders are not afraid to be different, and the fear of failure does not prevent them from trying to create a better world.

Second, it takes courage. Mary Frances Berry, former head of the U.S. Commission on Civil Rights, said, "The time when you need to do something is when no one else is willing to do it, when people are saying it can't be done." People who change the world know that courage means more than just saying what needs to be changed. It means deciding to be active in the effort to bring about change—no matter what it takes. They know they face numerous challenges: they may be criticized, made fun of, ignored, alienated from their friends and family, imprisoned, or even killed. But even though they may sometimes feel scared, they continue to pursue their vision of a better world.

Third, it takes dedication and patience. The Nobel Prize–winning scientist Marie Curie said, "One never notices what has been done; one can only see what remains to be done." People who change the world understand that change does not happen overnight. Changing the world is an ongoing process. They also know that while what they do is important, change depends on what others do as well. Their original vision may transform and evolve over time as it interacts with the visions of others and as circumstances change. And they know that the job is never finished. Each success brings a new challenge, and each failure yet another obstacle to overcome.

Finally, it takes inspiration. People who change the world find strength in the experiences and accomplishments of others who came before them. Sometimes these role models are family members or personal friends. Sometimes they are great women and men who have spoken out and written about their own struggles to change the world for the better. Reading books about these people—learning about their lives and reading their own words—can be a source of inspiration for future world-changers. For example, when I was young, someone gave me a book called *Girls' Stories of Great Women,* which provided me with ideas of what women had achieved in ways I had never dreamed of and in places that were very distant from my small town. It helped me to imagine what I could do with my life and to know that I myself could begin working toward my goals.

This series of books introduces us to women who have changed the world through their vision, courage, determination, and patience. Their stories reveal their struggles as world-changers against obstacles such as poverty, discrimination, violence, and injustice. Their stories also tell of their struggles as women to overcome the belief, which still exists in most societies, that girls are less capable than boys of achieving high goals, and that women are less likely than men to become leaders. These world-changing women often needed even more vision and courage than their male counterparts, because as women they faced greater discrimination and resistance. They certainly needed more determination and patience, because no matter how much they proved themselves, there were always people who were reluctant to take their leadership and their achievements seriously, simply because they were women.

These women and many others like them did not allow these challenges to stop them. As they fought on, they found inspiration in women as well as men—their own mothers and grandmothers, and the great women who had come before them. And now they themselves stand as an inspiration to young women and men all over the world.

The women whose lives are described in this series come from different countries around the world and represent a variety of cultures. Their stories offer insights into the lives of people in varying circumstances. In some ways, their lives may seem very different from the lives of most people in the United States. We can learn from these differences as well as from the things we have in common. Women often share similar problems and concerns about issues such as violence in their lives and in the world, or the kind of environment we are creating for the future. Further, the qualities that enable women to become leaders, and to make positive changes, are often the same worldwide.

The books in this series tell the stories of women who have fought for justice and worked for positive change within their own societies. These leaders have faced many different kinds of challenges and have responded to them in different ways. But one goal they all share is to promote "human rights"—the basic rights to which all human beings are entitled.

In 1948, the United Nations adopted the *Universal Declaration of Human Rights,* which outlines the rights of all people to freedom from slavery and torture, and to freedom of movement, speech, religion, and assembly, as well as rights of all people to social security, work, health, housing, education, culture, and citizenship. Further, it states that all people have the equal right to all these human rights, "without distinction of any kind such as race, color, sex, language . . . or other status."

In the United States, many of these ideas are not new to us. Some of them can be found in the first ten amendments to the U.S. Constitution, known as the Bill of Rights. Yet these ideals continually face many challenges, and they must be defended and expanded by every generation. They have been tested in this country, for example, by the Civil Rights movement to end racial discrimination and the movement to bring about equal rights for women. They continue to be tested even today by various individuals and groups who are fighting for greater equality and justice.

All over the world, women and men work for and defend the common goal of human rights for all. In some places these rights are severely violated. Tradition and prejudice as well as social, economic, and political interests

FOREWORD

often exclude women, in particular, from benefitting from these basic rights. Over the past decade, women around the world have been questioning why "women's rights" and women's lives have been deemed secondary to "human rights" and the lives of men. As a result, an international women's human rights movement has emerged, with support from organizations such as the Center for Women's Global Leadership, to challenge limited ideas about human rights and to alert all nations that "women's rights are human rights."

The following biography is the true story of a woman overcoming incredible obstacles—economic hardship, religious persecution, political oppression, and even the threat of violence and death—in order to peacefully achieve greater respect for human rights in her country. I am sure that you will find her story inspiring. I hope it also encourages you to join in the struggle to demand an end to all human rights violations—regardless of sex, race, class, or culture—throughout the world. And perhaps it will motivate you to become someone who just might change the world.

Charlotte Bunch
Founder and Executive Director
Center for Women's Global Leadership
Rutgers University

You can help to change the world now by establishing goals for yourself personally and by setting an example in how you live and work within your own family and community. You can speak out against unfairness and prejudice whenever you see it or hear it expressed by those around you. You can join an organization that is fighting for something you believe in, volunteer locally, or even start your own group in your school or neighborhood so that other people who share your beliefs can join you. Don't let anything or anyone limit your vision. Make your voice heard with confidence, strength, and dedication . . . and start changing the world today.

"We, the people of South Africa, declare for all our country and the world to know: that South Africa belongs to all who live in it, black and white, and that no government can justly claim authority unless it is based on the will of all the people."

—The Freedom Charter, 26 June 1955

Dr. Mamphela Ramphele, South African activist, physician, and educator.

Chapter 1
BANISHED!

Tzaneen! Mamphela Ramphele had never before heard of a place called Tzaneen. Now, tightly seated between two security officers, she was being taken there against her will. She was a prisoner! The car lurched through the bleak night. It was cold, and Mamphela, still wearing only the sleeveless dress and light sweater she'd had on when she was dragged out of the office and arrested earlier that day, shivered.

The triumphant words of Captain Schoeman still rang in her ears: "Well, Dr. Ramphele, good-bye, you b———!" Schoeman thought he had won, and in some ways, Ramphele was to discover, he had. She was being banished to a far-off, lonely piece of the country, a rural area with few trees, not enough water, and little hope for a better future. What's more, she was being sent away from the center of her life—away from her political activism, her medical clinic, and away from everyone who knew her, from family, from friends, from the man she loved. She was totally alone. If she tried to leave Tzaneen, she would be arrested.

It was 1977, and the white government of South Africa was cracking down. The worst racial violence and riots in South African memory had happened less than a year before. Black South Africans had risen up in protest against the government's system of racial segregation. They refused to go on being denied good schools, jobs, and the freedom to choose where to live. And they seemed to have a new awareness of their own strength, a new pride in themselves. They called it Black Consciousness. Mamphela could take some of the credit for that. She was part of the Black Consciousness movement.

Like other black South Africans her age, Mamphela had never known a world without apartheid. As a girl, she had seen black neighbors thrown out of their homes because they had argued with white authorities. She had slept on dirt floors and iron cots and all the while had kept on studying and learning and excelling in school. She had been born into a world that tried to restrict her education and her opportunities because she was black, and then added even more restrictions because she was female. Yet she had prevailed. She had won scholarships and attended college and medical school—an extraordinary achievement for a black woman. But for Mamphela, all this had been just the beginning.

She was not yet thirty years old, but already she had been in the inner circles that created the Black Consciousness movement in South Africa. She had developed a vision of a just future for black South Africans—a future of equality. Energetic and strong-willed, Mamphela had reached out to the people around her, becoming a leader in whatever she did. As a doctor, she had directed medical teams in poverty-stricken camps and townships, the areas outside cities where black South Africans were forced to live. She had organized a clinic that treated black South Africans with respect and dignity; for most of them, this was a first. Mamphela had been part of the team planning many student and activist projects, and she had led Black Consciousness conferences.

As a Black Consciousness leader, Mamphela believed that the road to liberation for black South Africans lay through empowerment. And this is the way she had led her life. She had helped people see their own strengths and feel their own power. And she believed that people who were empowered would never accept a system as insulting as apartheid. She was proving to be correct.

Now one part of Mamphela's life was coming to an end. Apartheid officials were sending her far away so she would have no more influence over people. But they were to discover that Mamphela would always find a way to influence and empower people. While banned, she would create the Ithuseng Community Health Centre, which would become both a respected medical clinic and a powerful resource center helping people start businesses and learn skills.

One day she would also write books. Her autobiography, *Across Boundaries*, would reveal her own history—the obstacles she overcame, as a black person and a woman, and the terrible losses she suffered, along with the triumphs she achieved. Her life story would also be a history of the Black Consciousness movement and the struggles to end apartheid. She would write other books too, exposing the effects that apartheid violence had on children, and the poverty that gripped the nation's black migrant workers.

She would later become the first black woman to run a university in South Africa, as the vice chancellor of the University of Cape Town. And finally, she would see the end of the hated system of apartheid and would help shape a new South Africa. She would be one of South Africa's most influential leaders.

But as the police drove her on into the night, Mamphela could not see any of this. She could barely see the road, and she did not know where it led or what lay ahead of her. Her mood was as dark as the night.

Chapter 2
GROWING UP UNDER APARTHEID

While Mamphela Aletta Ramphele was uttering her first cries in the middle of a hot summer afternoon on December 28, 1947, a new system, *apartheid*, was also being born. This new system would determine the course of Mamphela's life.

Mamphela, however, was not yet concerned about such things as apartheid. She was suffering through neonatal jaundice, a dangerous condition that affects some newborn babies, and she was simply trying to stay alive. She did survive, and she survived a bout of whooping cough at three months, too. These first months seemed to set the tone for Mamphela's life. Although she has never been an exceptionally strong or robust person physically, she has always possessed staying power—an inner strength that has carried her through difficulties, tragedies, and fears. Even through apartheid.

The birth of apartheid was celebrated by jubilant members of the victorious party—the all-white National Party. Whites had long held control of South Africa. But the National Party was the most conservative political group, and they promised to pass new, strict laws guaranteeing white rule. "Today South Africa belongs to us!" A white leader announced to the South African parliament in 1948. "We shall be introducing legislation . . . which we call apartheid. The separation between the races."

The National Party was known as the Afrikaner party because it was dominated by conservative white Afrikaners. It had won the elections by narrowly defeating the United Party, which was dominated by more liberal white South Africans. The white liberals were concerned about the upcoming political change and the new apartheid system. Black South Africans were fearful.

Mamphela, just a few months old, did not notice this major change in her country's government. In fact, she wouldn't notice it for quite some time. She lived in a small, isolated village in the northern Transvaal, the Kranspoort Mission Station. It was nestled at the foot of the Soutpansberg Mountains, a range that stretches across a section of northeastern South Africa just south of Zimbabwe. Mamphela's village received plenty of rain and was lush and

Victoria Falls, on the border of Zambia and Zimbabwe, is one of the most beautiful landscapes in the world, and is just one example of the many different natural environments of southern Africa. The waterfall is 350 feet high.

Mamphela's mother stands in front of their family home, at Uitkyk in northern South Africa, where Mamphela grew up.

green. Gardens grew luscious ripe vegetables, and orchards yielded abundant fruit. Water was plentiful, streams were full, and the rugged mountains were beautiful in the background. This was a good place to be a child. Mamphela had fields to play in and trees to climb.

Most of the people Mamphela knew in her village were black, but the village was run by a white dominee (minister) of the Dutch Reformed Church, the Reverend Lukas Van der Merwe. As with many villages, law enforcement, local government and the school were all controlled by the church, called "the mission" because of its missionary founders.

Mamphela's mother, Rangoato Rahab (Mahlaela) Ramphele, was a teacher, and her father, Pitsi Eliphaz Ramphele, was a teacher and the principal at the mission school. Because of this, the Ramphele family lived comfortably compared to many people in the village. Although their house had a mud floor, it also had three bedrooms. Mamphela recalls that for beds they "spread either straw mats or goatskins on the mud floor with a blanket placed on top." The children slept well on these floor beds. They also always had enough to eat,which meant that they were prosperous by local standards.

Mamphela's great-grandmother Koko Tsheola baby-sat the children while Mamphela's mother and father taught at the school. Koko Tsheola, Mamphela remembers, had a kind gentleness about her, and the children loved her. On many days, they would gather around her in the kitchen while she told them fascinating stories about her childhood. Then, if they asked, she'd tell them a folktale or two and sometimes a few riddles. Best of all, she gave the children spare change to buy candy at the local store. Life in such a household was full of excitement and contentment.

Once a year Mamphela's life would take an even more exciting turn: the annual visit to her father's family in Uitkyk. The homestead was about a thirty-mile trip, and it was a lively one because the family rode there in a wagon pulled by six mules. But it was when they arrived that the most amazing part of the trip began. This was when Mamphela's grandmother, Ramaesela Ramphele, would greet them with praise-singing.

Ramaesela would stride across the fields, her skirt blowing behind her in the hot, dry breeze. She would stand in the open and raise her voice to sing the family praises. And what a praise singer she was! Her Sotho words flowed in a rhythm and chant, rising and falling, rising and falling. Soon, Ramaesela would

Who are the South Africans?

South Africans today are a diverse mix of 41.2 million people. About 74 percent trace their heritage back to one of the ethnic groups that inhabited the land before the Europeans arrived—the Zulu, Xhosa, Swazi, Ndebele, and others. Each group has its own distinct history, culture, and language. White South Africans comprise about 14 percent of the population. They are divided between the Afrikaners, descended from Dutch, French, and German immigrants, and the English-speaking descendents of immigrants from the British Isles and other European nations. These Europeans arrived as settlers or as colonists, seeking to control the native people and resources for their own benefit. Much of South Africa was once a British colony, under the rule of Great Britain. But many whites stayed—and held on to power—after South Africa gained its independence in the early part of the twentieth century. About 3 percent of the South African population is of Asian descent, primarily immigrants from India, who arrived later than most of the Europeans. The remaining 9 percent of South Africans are of mixed racial heritage.

be dancing, and her singing and dancing would rise to a great crescendo of excitement. She sang the praises of the family's ancestors: Of Phoshiwa, Mamphela's paternal grandfather, she sang, *"O dutse leweng la nkwe ontse a shitisa nkwe go bopa"* ("Phoshiwa's bravery silenced even tigers"). And of Sethiba, Mamphela's maternal grandfather, she sang that he was "a handsome only child, a leader and warrior who blocked the white settlers' way." All great exploits were woven into the praises of those who had come before them, of those who were alive but not on hand, and then of those who were there listening that day. Mamphela was mesmerized.

According to custom, Ramaesela had to focus on the men's victories, but she was a woman with strong ideas of her own. She included some of the women in her praises too, and she included herself, in all her glory, in the center of her family's life. Mamphela

Traditional homes in some rural areas look like these round, thatched mud houses called rondavels. Mamphela's grandparents lived in rondavels.

learned early that she came from a long, proud line of strong and outspoken women.

Many things about Mamphela's vacation with her grandparents were different from life at home. Mamphela's grandfather's houses were built in a traditional style, with one tin-roofed house and several *rondavels* (round, thatched mud houses) all arranged around a central courtyard, or *lapa*.

Females and males were separated on her grandfather's land, so Mamphela wasn't allowed to play with her brothers as usual. She noticed, too, that on this vacation her father relaxed with the men, but her mother worked harder than ever. Tradition demanded that she cook and serve meals to whomever visited, and since the family was in town for a vacation, everyone stopped by to chat and share a meal. When the meal was served the men ate first, then the older women, and finally the children.

Some of the old traditions annoyed Mamphela's mother, and she was famous in the family for putting an end to one of them. Women were not allowed to help slaughter an animal, and afterwards they were not allowed near the fire where men gathered to boil the favored parts, such as the spleen, liver, and heart, for themselves. Women had to wait until the men brought them meat to cook for the children's dinner. So, the women would wait—and wait. And as the women waited, the men would sit around their fire chatting and munching, and filling up on the tender meat. One evening, Mamphela's mother had had enough of waiting. "She calmly walked up to the men's fireplace," recalls Mamphela, "and carried away the pot." Then she dished it out to the women

Where is South Africa?

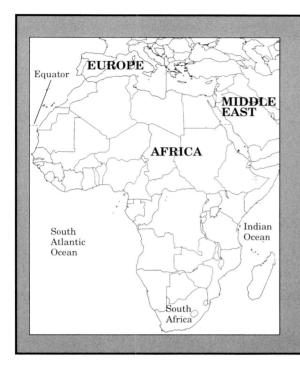

South Africa, the southern-most nation in Africa, is 471,440 square miles (about twice the size of Texas). Situated at the tip of Africa, between two oceans, its climate varies from warm and temperate to subtropical, to arid, with bush-filled hillsides, pasturelands, farms, and parched deserts. South Africa is home to some of the world's richest diamond and gold mines, along with many other minerals, forests, and fertile land. Cattle and sheep ranching and farming support its rural population. Its cities are centers for international trade and industry. Much of these resources, however, are controlled by a few—still mostly white—citizens, and the majority of South Africans are poor.

and children. The men were "stunned." This had *never* happened before.

Mamphela's mother changed tradition that day. From then on, the men were more cooperative. Her mother "had liberated both men and women," says Mamphela, and taught them a lesson, too: Ancient traditions can be shaped into new traditions that honor all.

In Mamphela's own home, back at the mission village, the children shared the chores equally because both of Mamphela's parents were very busy. The family's focus was on school and achievement. Mamphela herself was eager to start school. But when she was old enough, her mother said no.

Mamphela would have to stay home for another year. Koko Tsheola was getting older, and didn't have enough strength to watch the babies by herself. It was a tear-filled day, Mamphela recalled many years later. But she made the best of her situation, inventing games for her baby brothers, Sethiba and Phoshiwa, and playing outdoors.

Mamphela started school the next year, and, although she didn't realize it, the new apartheid laws were already affecting her life. One of the most infamous laws, the Bantu Education Act of 1953 made sure that black children would receive an inferior education to that of white children. Black children would learn arithmetic but not algebra, and basic science but not chemistry or physics. They

What was Apartheid?

Apartheid separated South Africans according to their racial and ethnic heritage. It was a political system that officially began in 1948 and that reflected the prejudice of white South Africans in the government and a large part of the white population.

Apartheid divided South Africans into four groups: 1) the "Native" group, later known as the "Bantu" group and then the "Black" group, included black South Africans; 2) the "Coloured" group included people of mixed black African and European heritage; 3) the "Asian" group included people of Asian descent, including Indian; 4) the "White" group included people of Caucasian European heritage. A person's opportunities, privileges, and rights in all phases of life depended on her classification. Black South Africans could not vote, go to most schools or hospitals, or choose where to live. "Asians" and "Coloureds" were given more rights than "Blacks," but still far fewer than "Whites."

But apartheid was more than simple racism. It was economics, too. Under apartheid, white South Africans controlled the nation's rich gold and diamond mines. They also owned virtually all of South Africa's industries and businesses. Apartheid guaranteed them a cheap labor force with few rights: black South Africans.

After the Bantu Education Act was passed in 1953, outlaw schools were set up by families to teach their children in English. Most were quickly shut down by the apartheid government. Now, all South African schools may choose the language they teach in, as well as what cultures and religions they want to reflect.

would learn elementary reading and writing, much of it in tribal languages, and just enough English or Afrikaans to communicate with a boss. Dr. Hendrik F. Verwoerd, the minister of native affairs, said black South Africans should never be taught enough to be executives and leaders because they would never become those things. When he explained the law to teachers, he said, black children "should not be shown green pastures where they would never be allowed to graze."

Black parents were horrified. Without a proper education, their children would never rise out of poverty. When the law first was passed, women fought back, recalls Albertina Sisulu, who became a leader in the struggle against apartheid. "We withdrew our children from the schools and they were

How have black South Africans fought back throughtout history?

In the seventeenth, eighteenth, and nineteenth centuries, white Europeans arrived in South African lands and began to restrict the native black population, taking away their land and rights. From the start, black South Africans fought back. Indeed, an early people, the Khoikhoi, waged a mighty battle until their defeat in 1677. As the Europeans then forced their way further inland, the Xhosa and Zulu tried to stop them. They fought valiantly, but in the end were defeated by the heavily armed invaders.

More recently, black South Africans protested segregation with demonstrations and strikes. In 1913, when the South African government tried to enact a law that made women carry passes, the women marched and won the day. Black South Africans demonstrated again and again, attempting to convince the white-controlled government to grant blacks equality.

closed," she said, reports author Ann Oosthuizen. "We employed our own teachers and went on giving our children the right type of education." But the government shut these outlaw schools down simply by refusing to officially recognize them. This way, children who graduated from them could not go on to other schools or universities.

Still, black South Africans did not sit back and accept this or other new, oppressive laws. The African National Congress (ANC), a group demanding equal rights for all South Africans, helped organize the nationwide Defiance Campaign. Led by Nelson Mandela and other dynamic young leaders, thousands of black South Africans attended mass rallies. Many burned the despised identity passes they were forced to carry. Thousands more participated in "stay-at-homes", or strikes, stopping all kinds of work to demonstrate the importance of their labor to the nation's economy. They hoped that the government would repeal the new apartheid laws. By the end of the year, however, it was clear that the government was not responding to the people's campaign as hoped.

Instead, the government became even more repressive. Police arrested nearly 8,500 people who participated in the Defiance Campaign. Numerous leaders were put under house arrest, and others were banned. The government, in short, reacted to the campaign by trying to break the spirit of the rebellion and of the people. But the ANC became even stronger during this period. In 1952, its membership increased from 7,000 to 100,000. Black South Africans were clearly supporting Nelson Mandela and other ANC leaders, including Albert Luthuli, Walter Sisulu, and Oliver Tambo.

News of the Defiance Campaign and the government's inhumane treatment of the people filtered back to Mamphela's rural village, but not to Mamphela herself. She was, after all, just a small child, and children were "to be seen and not heard". Mamphela's life continued, with home, chores, play, and school.

Two children share a ride on their donkey. In South Africa, children have an important role in their families, helping with chores, caring for livestock, and looking after younger brothers and sisters.

Chapter 3

AN UNCONVENTIONAL GIRL

Mamphela's father was her teacher, and she remembers him in *Across Boundaries* as "a wonderful teacher who enthused his pupils with the joy of learning." He also waged his own quiet defiance campaign against the Bantu Education Act.

The act required him to teach in Sotho, the language of the region's ethnic group. For most of the year, however, he taught in English. He believed that if his students knew only Sotho, they would be cut off not only from the white community, but also from many of the other black communities of South Africa. This is what the creaters of apartheid wanted: to divide black South Africans into separate, small, manageable groups.

Mamphela's father also defied the government's order to teach only the basic information included in the official course outline prepared by the Ministry of Native Affairs. According to the required outline, students learned about white heroes in history. It was designed, like the Bantu Education Act, to make black South Africans feel inferior, and to keep them from being able to compete with white South Africans. Mamphela's father, however, proudly taught his students more advanced theories and ideas.

Schoolwork was only part of Mamphela's responsibility at the mission school. Students also had *huiswerk* (housework) in the dominee's house and yard, and he was a harsh taskmaster. Mamphela

What are the languages of South Africa?

South Africa lists eleven official languages. Two of these are imported. Afrikaans developed from the Dutch language used and transformed by Dutch, German, Belgian, and French immigrants. English arrived with British colonists. The other nine languages are native to South Africa. Of these, the most widely used are Zulu, Xhosa, and Pedi. The others include Sotho, Tswana, Tsonga, Swazi, Venda, Ndebele.

Most black South Africans speak their own native language as a first language, but are bilingual, or even trilingual. English has been the preferred second language. In addition, despite apartheid's efforts to keep black South Africans divided into their own ethnic sections, the people have long maintained fluid relations. So many black South Africans trace their heritage back to more than one native group and speak more than one tribal language.

recalls the hours spent sweeping the open spaces between the fruit trees around his house, the students rustling along under the trees, sweeping with brooms made of bushes—the fruit hanging ripe and within reach above their heads. Such temptation! Yet, Mamphela and her friends never touched it. "The dominee was a merciless man," she later wrote, and he had the power to expel entire families from the village. Then where would they go? What would they eat? They would be homeless. And as head of the mission school, the dominee was her parents' boss. He had such power!

The fears and feelings of powerlessness that Mamphela felt as she swept the dominee's yard were similar to the feelings of almost all black South Africans. Their lives, whether they were children or adults, were controlled and dominated by rules made by whites. Adult women and men were addressed as "girl" and "boy" by most white South Africans, and could risk losing their jobs by demanding respect. They could be legally fired or sent away to homelands—poor, rural areas far from cities, like reservations.

Black South Africans coped with discrimination in many ways. One was by choosing an extra, European name to be used in public and in school, a name that was easier for non-Africans to pronounce than African language names. Mamphela's public name was Aletta. This is what she was called in public and by friends until, as an adult, she rejected it and insisted on being called Mamphela.

Despite daily reminders of the white world, Mamphela, living in a rural mission community with few white people, spent much of her childhood isolated from racial conflicts. Many events filled her young days. Christmas and New Year celebrations were joyous, festive times. They fell during South Africa's summer. The children would be on school break, and the men who had been working as migrant laborers in mines or on distant farms would be home to spend the holiday with their families. Mamphela remembers that everyone decorated their houses with "fresh, colorful mud, . . . paper ribbons and balloons." Most also strung colorful strips of fabric in their doorways. Competitions were held for children's church choirs, and dancing was ongoing.

It could seem at times like these that Mamphela's small village was untouched by outside influences—that it would continue on forever centered around its strict Dutch Reformed Church, the dominee, the school, and the festivities. It could seem that way to a small girl of seven, anyway. But of course, it could not remain isolated. There came the day, in 1955, when the villagers rebelled against one of the Dominee's decisions.

Black South Africans make up about 70 percent of the population and about 75 percent of the workforce. Under apartheid, they were expected to live on 14 percent of the land. A typical rural family's income might come from raising sheep for wool, or from farming wheat, sugar, or fruit.

As Mamphela later described, it was a small rebellion, but one that reflected the mood of the nation. It started with the death of an elderly woman. Her daughter wanted to bury her in the church's graveyard, but the dominee refused: the elderly woman was not a Christian. The villagers buried her there anyway. This infuriated the dominee. His villagers had disobeyed him—unthinkable! He called in the police. He also had a shouting match in the street with some of the villagers, and some of the women actually called him "Lukas," his first name! That was highly disrespectful, as they were supposed to address him always as Moruti (Preacher).

Security police, who were trained to protect the government by suppressing protests nationwide, arrested many of the villagers. They beat several villagers while they had them in custody. Yet the people would not give in. Neither would the dominee. He evicted two-thirds of the village residents, sending some of them off with just the clothes on their backs, many of them with nowhere to go.

At the time, even young Mamphela could see that something was happening in South Africa. Black people were not bowing to apartheid; instead, they were rising up and challenging the white South African government.

In 1955, some 3,000 delegates representing groups from across the nation met near Soweto, a township outside Johannesburg, for a Congress of the People. Nelson Mandela, though banned at the time, attended. Albert Luthuli presided for the African National Congress. The Congress of Democrats, a group of white South Africans opposed to apartheid, attended; so did the Coloured People's Congress, the

How did the government create Apartheid?

The government passed several laws to create apartheid. One law limited black South Africans to seventy-two hours in urban areas unless they were employed. This broke up families; unemployed spouses were forced to live in the homelands, or reservations, far outside cities. Another law required all black South Africans to carry identification cards (passbooks). These books had to be stamped by employers and carried at all times to prove the pass-holders' right to be in the area. When caught by the police without updated stamps in their passbooks, hundreds of thousands of people were arrested or sent to the homelands·

Laws also prohibited blacks from owning land outside the homelands, another attempt to keep them away from urban white communities. Other laws made interracial marriage illegal and segregated public places, such as beaches and theaters. Because of these and other apartheid laws, separation of the races was soon quite complete.

South African Indian Congress, and many others. All groups had a united purpose: to find a new vision for South Africa, one to replace apartheid.

Banners proclaimed "Freedom in Our Lifetime, Long Live the Struggle." Participants held a new document in hand, the Freedom Charter. As they read it and voted for it, they felt new hope for South Africa. The Freedom Charter spelled out goals of equality and fairness for all South Africans—black, white, Asian, and "Coloured." But as they were voting to support the Freedom Charter, the delegates were suddenly surrounded by police. The police announced that they suspected all the delegates of treason, and they recorded the names of everyone there. Often, if people who spoke out had not broken any law, they would be accused of treason, meaning that they had threatened the safety of the current government. This excuse was used to discourage protests and to lock up activists indefinitely. This harassment angered those attending the Congress of the People, and made most of them even more determined to thwart apartheid.

The government, meanwhile, began to enforce the pass law for women that had been enacted in 1952. Women had already made their feelings about passes clear back in 1913 when the government had tried to make them carry passes to keep track of where each person was allowed to live, work, and travel. Women had been demonstrating against apartheid along with men since 1952, but now here was the apartheid government again saying women would have to carry passes.

Women responded angrily. In 1955, they protested throughout the country, with 2,000 marching on the parliament building in Pretoria. Through the next year, despite continued protest and unrest, the government enforced the pass laws. Still, the women did not give up.

In 1956, the Federation of South African Women organized an even grander protest than the first one.

In 1956, 20,00 women marched to the Union Building, the office of the prime minister in Pretoria, in order to protest the passbook laws.

This time, more than 20,000 women marched on the government buildings in Pretoria. They arrived by train, by taxi, by foot, by whatever means it took to get there, many of them carrying children on their backs. Each woman carried a letter of protest with her. They marched to the offices of the prime minister, Johannes Strijdom (who left the building for the day), and they dropped all 20,000 protest letters on his doorstep. Lillian Ngoyi, one of the leaders of the protest, announced to the women gathered before her: "The prime minister was not there. He has run away from the women."

To demonstrate their solidarity, the women stood in silence, arms raised in protest, for thirty minutes. Then Ngoyi led them in singing the anthem of African protesters, "Nkosi Sikelel' iAfrika" ("God Bless Africa"). It was an emotional moment. Years later, anti-apartheid leader Helen Joseph recalled the day for writer Diana Russell. "I've never heard it sung like that before or since," she said. "Never ever!" The women's voices rose passionately, in unison, in hope. Then they sang a song written for the occasion. They sang, "Strijdom, you have struck a rock. You have tampered with the women." These lyrics became well known throughout South Africa as an expression of the strength of women's resolve.

Unfortunately, the government still was not listening. In 1956, Helen Joseph and Lillian Ngoyi were among the 156 people arrested by police for signing the Freedom Charter. The list included Nelson Mandela, and all 156 were charged with high treason. Though all were ultimately acquitted, their trial lasted for five years.

Who is Nelson Mandela and what is the ANC?

Nelson Rolihlahla Mandela, born in 1918, became an international symbol of the battle to end South African apartheid and played a major role in ending the violence and injustice in South Africa. Although imprisoned for twenty-seven years, he has always been recognized around the world as a leader of the African National Congress (ANC). The ANC is the political group that organized resistance to apartheid.

Mandela, an attorney, joined the ANC in 1942 and immediately began to spread the ANC message of protest against apartheid. During the 1950s he was banned, arrested, and imprisoned for various political protests and sabotage.

In 1961, the ANC formed a military arm, the Umkhonto we Sizwe (Spear of the Nation) with Mandela as its commander-in-chief. Its primary goal was to sabotage public facilities and to disrupt South Africa so much that the nation would become ungovernable. Just three years later, the government convicted seven of the ANC's top Umkhonto we Sizwe's leaders, including Mandela, of high treason. All were sentenced to life in prison, and the ANC was outlawed in South Africa.

During the next twenty-seven years in prison, Mandela never stopped waging a battle for racial equality in South Africa. Though behind bars, he grew to be the central commander of ANC protest in the country; Oliver Tambo, who had escaped to exile in England, was the party's external leader. Millions of people across South Africa and the world supported the two leaders in their struggles against apartheid.

Young Nelson Mandela leaves the court after the prolonged treason trial of the late 1950s ended. The ANC was made illegal, and Mandela went into hiding after the trial.

The rest of the world was beginning to notice South Africa's blatantly racist policies, and to react. At first the news filtered out slowly. Most people had not heard about the cramped, flimsy shacks in squatter camps that black South Africans were living in because they had nowhere else to go. But then the apartheid government caught the attention of international media when it bulldozed whole blocks of homes in the squatter camp of Sophiatown and forced thousands of people off to the homelands. An international outcry went up following the destruction of the camp. South Africa did not waver from apartheid, however, and instead passed more laws to limit the lives of its black citizens.

Black South Africans continued to protest. In Durban, a seaport town on the east coast of South Africa, unrest lasted for several months in 1959. The next year, some 30,000 protesters attended an anti-pass demonstration in Cape Town; two people were

After a women's anti-pass demonstration in Durban in 1959, the police violently attack protestors. Women eventually succeeded, and pass laws for women were abandoned.

killed when police advanced on the crowd with batons swinging and the demonstration turned into a riot.

But it was a demonstration at Sharpeville in March of 1960 that revealed the true violence of apartheid. The demonstration was organized by the Pan Africanist Congress (PAC), a group that split off from the ANC. Several thousand protesters, carrying signs saying "Freedom in our time" and "Freedom and Justice Not Pass Laws," surrounded the small Sharpeville police station. The protesters waved their signs, sang protest songs, and did the protest "jog"—a rhythmic, running movement to the chants and songs.

The protesters were unarmed. Nevertheless, the police responded with deadly force. There were only seventy-five police, and they later excused their reaction as panic at being so outnumbered. They leveled their weapons at the crowd and fired. They fired more than 700 shots. Even as the people turned and ran, the police kept firing. In the end, sixty-nine people—women, men, and children—lay dead, most of them shot in the back as they were fleeing. At least 186 people were wounded; some say the number was closer to 400.

The Sharpeville massacre, as it became known, touched off a series of events. Countries around the world condemned the South African government for the killings. The United Nations called on South Africa to mend its ways. South African leader Albert Luthuli burned his pass in protest and called on others to follow his lead. In Langa, near Cape Town, 50,000 protesters rallied. Rioting broke out across the nation, and the apartheid government declared a state of emergency, passing laws giving police powers to arrest and to hold people without evidence.

In the same year, 1960, black South African leader Albert Luthuli, though under house arrest for his political activities, won the Nobel Peace Prize, which is awarded annually for work toward world peace and justice. In 1961, the United Nations General Assembly voted to sanction South Africa, a move that meant that the rest of the world was being urged to stop investing money in, trading goods with, or establishing businesses in South Africa. This could cripple South Africa's economy, hitting the government where it hurt—in the pocketbook. Clearly, white South Africa was losing respect throughout the world.

Mamphela's rural mission town was quite isolated, but even so, her family was personally affected by some of the unrest. Her older sister, Mashadi, was expelled from boarding school the next year because she refused to celebrate when South Africa declared itself fully independent from Great Britain. Most black South Africans were not celebrating this event. They believed that they had more hope for freedom under Great Britain's rule than they would have when left entirely under South Africa's. Thousands were protesting, with demonstrations in Pretoria, Johannesburg, Cape Town, and elsewhere.

Mamphela, then fourteen years old, was not told about most of the unrest. She was focused instead on moving away from home to boarding school, and was hoping for a challenging education. But she was disappointed when she arrived at Bethesda Normal School. It was old and shabby. The girls slept on iron spring beds with uncomfortable mattresses in a bleak dormitory. And even worse was the food. It was both tasteless and meager. Porridge formed the base of every meal, with a potato or cabbage added for lunch, and a cup of non-dairy cocoa for dinner. A couple of times a week, the children would get meat and bread with their meals. And even if they ate all of these meals, they would still be hungry.

Mamphela's classes were taught chiefly in Afrikaans by white teachers. The teachers, Mamphela wrote, were "keenly interested in the success of their students," but still kept a wall between the black students and themselves. Students must always know their place. The school also had *huiswerk* similar to the chores back at the mission school. But now Mamphela began to realize the real purpose of this labor: it was "to remind students that education was not an escape route from the inferior position blacks were 'destined' to occupy," she later wrote in *Across Boundaries*.

The school, like South Africa in general, could be a confusing place for a young student. Having friends helped make sense of it, and Mamphela made some close friends while there. She and three other girls became a high-spirited foursome. They sat together in class, joked, chatted, and spent as much time together as they could. They saw themselves as unconventional. Just the fact that they were a mixed group of country and city girls was breaking with the traditions of their day. (Country girls were warned to stay away from city girls, who would lead them astray.) The fact that the foursome laughed aloud and questioned the system at the school made them downright modern.

These girls attend a mission school like the one where Mamphela studied as a child. In Mamphela's time, far fewer girls and than boys attended school, but today girls' and women's educational opportunities are steadily increasing.

Even more unconventional was Mamphela's decision upon graduation. She chose to take college preparatory courses. Only one other girl and only a handful of boys from her school were heading for universities. Most of the girls who were good students would go into teaching or nursing. Boys who did well in school might choose teaching or police work; others would become migrant farm or mine workers.

Mamphela did not want to teach. Black female teachers were paid even less than black male teachers, and *their* pay was lower than pay for white teachers. Mamphela's sister, Mashadi, in training as a nurse, said that black nurses were treated like maids. So it became obvious to Mamphela that the best thing to be was a doctor. Being a doctor "could offer me the greatest professional freedom and satisfaction," she says. "It was not the desire to serve

What opportunities existed for black South Africans under apartheid?

Apartheid strictly limited all opportunities for blacks. The only work available to most men was low-paying migrant labor on farms, in the mines, or in other industries. The jobs open to women were as maids or nannies for white households, which paid even less than the men's jobs.

Laws also restricted black South Africans from being promoted above skilled labor. Educated black South Africans could, however, become professionals, such as teachers or nurses, serving the segregated black communities. They could also run small businesses such as restaurants and shops for black customers. But it was virtually impossible for blacks to become rich, illegal for them to own their own homes, and dangerous for them to forget even for a moment any of apartheid's many restrictions. All black people were expected to treat white people with humble and exaggerated respect.

which influenced my career choice, but the passion for freedom to be my own mistress."

She was, indeed, making a wise decision, one that would lead to the most freedom a black woman in South Africa could hope for as long as apartheid was in effect. It was an unusual decision, however. Very few black South African males became medical doctors. And females? Why, you could count them on one hand.

At school, Mamphela, like all the students, had been kept as isolated as possible from the politics of South Africa. The teachers did not want students to know about Nelson Mandela, about the African National Congress, or about all of the unrest and protest in South Africa. It was the end of 1964, and while Mamphela had been quietly studying off in her rural school, police had been arresting and holding in jail thousands of black South Africans. About this time, too, Nelson Mandela was imprisoned. He would not emerge for twenty-seven years.

Chapter 4

A POLITICAL EDUCATION

Mamphela stood with the other departing students in front of Dominee Lukas Van der Merwe. It was January 1965, and she was leaving for a new school. The dominee was angry at her choice of profession, Mamphela recalled in *Across Boundaries*. The dominee's own daughter had wanted to become a doctor but had failed. Now this thin, black girl aspired to be a doctor? It was "a pipe dream," he said. Mamphela would never make it, he predicted angrily. Never. She was black, and a female at that. There was no chance.

Mamphela ignored this discouragement and, at the age of seventeen, attended a new boarding school. On her arrival, she saw how the Bantu Education Act had limited her. Because she had been taught no algebra, the concept of multiplying and finding square roots of an "alphabet" of factors threw her. Luckily, she and a few other black students in the same position found a retired teacher who was willing to teach them algebra.

Two other teachers also took an interest in Mamphela's education. Both white and both members of the National Party (the party responsible for apartheid), they showed Mamphela surprising generosity and support. Partly because of them, she did well in her classes and would be prepared the next year to move on to a university.

Interestingly, the professors' support for Mamphela did not mean that they were abandoning their belief

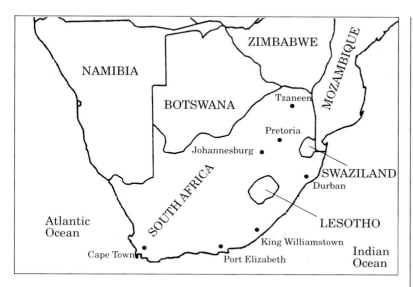

When Mamphela Ramphele left her small village to go to school, she began learning more about her country. She would live in many different places, in the country and in the cities, from rural Tzaneen way up north to metropolitan Cape Town on the southwestern coast.

in apartheid. They did not support equality for black South Africans, but they could safely take an interest in a young woman who would one day be assigned to a black hospital to treat only black patients. Mamphela, not yet a political activist, recalled later that one of them even pinned a National Party button on her shirt one day. And she, ignorant of its racist symbolism, wore it.

Mamphela studied hard and placed at the top of her class. She was a loner, she recalls, and quite content to keep to herself. Her classmates, she deduced, probably found her aloof, maybe even "stuck-up." Some were intimidated by her. But finally one of them, Dick Mmabane, mustered enough courage to talk to her. "He confessed that he had expected me to dismiss him at first base," remembers Mamphela. But she fell madly in love instead. "My heart leapt into a happy rhythm each time we went out together," she says.

How was apartheid enforced?

Despite the fact that blacks are the majority of the population, white South Africans were able to enforce apartheid because they had complete control of South Africa's resources. They ran the government, the courts, the businesses, the military, and the police. They had both the money and the military power to enforce apartheid.

When blacks mounted protests against apartheid, the government granted its police greater and greater powers. New laws allowed police to jail people without evidence or trial (to detain them), and to use force to obtain information. Over the years, the police detained hundreds of thousands of protesters. They mistreated many, and tortured and killed some.

Dick Mmabane, like Mamphela, was a top student. In fact, he was chosen to speak at the school's farewell dance at the end of 1966. He was Mamphela's date for the event. She, wearing a powder blue, short-sleeved suit and black high heels, looked quite grown up that evening, which was appropriate. She was now moving into the next phase of her life: adulthood and university studies.

Meanwhile, the violence across South Africa had become a revolution. The government, using the powers granted them under a 1963 law, was "detaining" thousands of people—putting them in jail for ninety days without charging them with a crime.

Mamphela, still somewhat sheltered from the politics of her country and from the revolution that was taking place, went off to the University of the North in Pietersburg to begin her pre-med studies. Dick Mmabane was attending the same university. His studies took him to the law department; hers took her to the science laboratories. Like the schools Mamphela had attended before, the University of the North kept its students as isolated from politics as possible. Although it accepted black students, it was rigidly apartheid. Indeed, the registrar proudly announced in Afrikaans, *"My vel is my graad"* ("My skin is my degree"), meaning that the white color of his skin was all that he needed to qualify him for his job. Black students were segregated into separate dormitory sections of the campus and into black-only classes.

While student groups on other campuses were actively discussing politics, there were only social clubs at this university, so there were no protests against apartheid. Mamphela focused on passing the four classes needed for entrance into the University of Natal Medical School, the only medical school accepting black students without special approval from the government.

The year was both carefree and sad for Mamphela, and though she did not know it at the time, this was to be her last isolated and non-political year. In her free time she relaxed with Dick Mmabane. But she also witnessed the death of her father from cancer.

The family said farewell to Mamphela's father in a combination of traditional African and European-style funeral rituals. Relatives gathered at the family home in Uitkyk, holding an all-night vigil, with singing and preaching. They slaughtered an ox in Sotho tradition, and also held a service in the Dutch Reform Church tradition.

Back at school, Mamphela then ran into what looked like a major roadblock to her ambition: her chemistry professor. "There was no doubt in his mind," Mamphela would write, "that 'Bantus' could not master chemistry, and he made it his mission to prove this."

In *Across Boundaries*, Mamphela relates the story of this openly hostile professor. "He would breeze into the classroom—his cold blue eyes not making contact with anyone, but emitting sparks of hatred whenever one attracted his attention or dared to ask a question." He lectured from "old scraps of notes . . . visibly yellowing from age." But he saved his meanest trick for the complex chemistry formulas students needed to learn. He wrote them rapidly on the chalkboard, and as he wrote with one hand, he would follow with an eraser in the other—erasing the formula as soon as he wrote it! Students scrambled anxiously to keep up, and none succeeded. Instead, they formed a mutual help system. Students from previous semesters donated their notes, hoping that in combination students could piece together the information they needed.

This professor was an extreme example of the hostility that black South African students could face in university classrooms. His class was required for all science majors. Without his class, students could not go through the gate to medical school, and thereby on to becoming doctors. Therefore, he held the key to the gateway to further studies. He was a "gatekeeper" who, like many South Africans in positions of power, determined peoples' fate. Though all systems have "gateways," the problem for black South Africans was that the gatekeepers for their ambitions were almost always white—and some did their utmost to halt any black progress through the gates toward success and possible equality. Mamphela, fortunately, passed Professor De Villiers' class, and squeezed through the "gate," along with a few other students. She was ready to move on to the Natal Medical School, in the eastern seacoast city of Durban.

The University of Natal was a surprise. By this time, Mamphela, twenty years old, had lived away from home for six years, first in boarding schools and then at the university; she had also spent vacation weeks with Mmabane's family in Johannesburg. She felt quite sophisticated, but these students were more so! People spoke out against apartheid here! Indeed, the campus was liberal and encouraged active student politics. Mamphela quickly met a group of politically active, intellectual black South Africans.

These students were leaders in the Students Representative Council (SRC), a group that challenged apartheid and sought changes in South African politics. They also questioned the tactics that had been used by activists in the past. The group included a charismatic, handsome young man who would become important in Mamphela's life: Steve Biko. He was the leader of the group and had new ideas on how to fight apartheid.

Steve Biko argued that black South Africans needed to separate themselves into a black-only party. He said that black South Africans had to learn a new, deep appreciation of themselves as themselves—not as compared to white people. They had to see themselves not as "non-Europeans" or "non-whites" but as blacks. In the past, he explained, the measurement of people's worth was always the white community. White people were considered normal, usual, and correct—"the norm." Black South Africans needed to become their own norm. They needed to lead their own political movement.

As a form of protest, many people publicly burned the passbooks that the government required people living in townships to carry.

This was radical thinking.

At first Mamphela just listened as the arguments and debates raged around her. This was all new to her, but her scientific mind immediately grasped the meanings. Steve, she realized, could see an end to apartheid. He saw the path to that end as being through black self-confidence, self-reliance, and dignity—through the concept of Black Consciousness.

Steve Biko was a natural leader, both charming and intelligent. Father Aelred Stubbs, an Anglican priest and fellow activist, describes him as a man whose "soul was in his eyes." Steve was also an eloquent speaker who presented his arguments with quiet passion. By 1969, he and his followers were forming a new group, the all-black South African Students' Organization (SASO), founded on the idea of Black Consciousness. The organization would raise the self-respect of the black South African population. That was step one. The next step would be to assert black South Africans' demands for equal treatment under the law and for a political voice.

Mamphela was soon drawn into political activism. She became part of the weekend parties, the all-night discussions, and the campus get-togethers. Soon, she found herself going through a personal change. She went from an innocent and uninformed country girl to "a person who became alive to the vast possibilities which life has to offer."

The discussions were a political education. She learned the history of black heroes who fought European settlers, and the history of black struggle against the laws that restricted their freedom. She began to see her own role in apartheid: as long as she accepted its policies, she helped preserve it.

SASO, of which Mamphela Ramphele was a local branch chairperson, was founded by Steve Biko and became a nationwide organization. In contrast to the ANC's "non-racialism" approach to politics, SASO focused on developing activism for and by blacks.

Along with other activists, including Steve Biko and Barney Pityana, Mamphela listened to tapes of Malcolm X, which were censored and illegal in South Africa. Together, the students read the Reverend Martin Luther King's speeches and essays, which were also illegal. They discussed the Civil Rights Movement in the United States. They had long, serious discussions about Black Consciousness and the best methods of changing South Africa. But they also had fun times, "sharing jokes, and also singing and dancing," says Mamphela. She was soon speaking up in these informal groups and stating her own opinions. She was learning to be assertive, and learning how to hold her own in a heated debate. She was developing a new sense of her own strong, black womanhood.

She took a look at the smooth-haired wig she had always worn on special occasions, and threw it away. She accepted her short, "boyish" hair as her personal, African style. She also dropped the white European name, Aletta, that she had used throughout her school years. She wore jeans and hot pants. Before long, she was fully embracing the rebellious student culture of the 1960s. She was a student activist.

She recalls that she "spent many late nights helping Steve." She especially helped him with his political essays, and the two soon became great friends. Before long, it was obvious to all around them that the friendship was developing into a romance. Mamphela, however, reports that she tried to ignore the attraction. She was unavailable, she told herself and others. She had a boyfriend, Dick Mmabane, who was waiting for her and who was pressuring her to marry him.

Life for Mamphela was more complicated now than it had ever been before. It was also more full of promise and possibility. She and the student activists felt that they were making a difference. But while she was succeeding in politics, Mamphela found that other parts of her life were in trouble. First, some of her schoolwork was slipping. Politics and SASO activities had replaced school as her priority; consequently, she was not at the top of her class. Second, there was her friendship with Steve Biko. The sparks between them became impossible to ignore. Third, not surprisingly, there were problems in her relationship with Dick Mmabane.

Mamphela and Steve "conducted a semi-platonic friendship," says Mamphela, "which frequently 'degenerated' into passion." Mamphela was torn. What was she to do? Mamphela was forced to admit that she had fallen in love with Steve Biko, who shared her concerns and passions. Yet she had made promises to Dick. The two men pressured her, Dick

Mamphela Ramphele and Steve Biko wait outside the court building in Port Elizabeth during his trial. Activists against apartheid were often subjected to long trials as a form of intimidation.

pressing her to marry him, and Steve urging her to reconsider marriage. Dick sent Mamphela instructions; Steve sent her love poems.

Over Christmas break in 1969, Mamphela had to make a decision. She visited Dick and his family as she had promised. She thought she was a changed woman. And indeed, she did speak her mind and was politically sophisticated. But she had not completely changed. She still had some feelings for Dick, and those feelings led to one of her biggest personal mistakes.

Dick's relatives had already begun the marriage process. They had formally visited her family, and had offered the customary *lobola* (bride wealth) to Mamphela's grandfather. He "did not believe in the custom of *lobola*," says Mamphela, but had accepted a small gift as a "token." The fact that the older gen-

> ## How are women seeking equality in the home?
>
> Built into most cultures—from North America to Africa—are traditions that pass a young woman on from the protection of her father's home to that of her husband's. Many women today recognize that the "protection" can really be a restriction, creating dependence in a woman's life when she seeks independence and growth. Women across the world are questioning such restrictive traditions.
>
> In South Africa, one tradition women are questioning is *Lobola*, the price paid by the groom to the bride's family. Lydia Kompe, a South African activist, explains *lobola* to journalist Diana Russell: *Lobola* "used to bring two families together," she says. Today, though, *lobola* is often seen as purchasing the woman. Indeed, Mark Mathabane, in his memoir, *Kaffir Boy*, reports that his father, when angry, told his mother: "I bought you! I own you. Your duty is to look after my children, cook for me, and do what I say."
>
> Lydia Kompe and others have spoken out to try to put an end to *lobola*, but the practice is still popular.

eration of the family was involved added tremendous pressure on Mamphela to agree to marry Dick.

"I resigned myself to my fate," says Mamphela, "and even allowed myself to get excited." The wedding took place immediately. By the time school resumed, Mamphela was a married woman.

Chapter 5
BLACK CONSCIOUSNESS

So much was happening for Mamphela, and most of it was taking place outside of the classroom. The students weren't just discussing change anymore, they were making changes—taking their ideas to the people.

Mamphela's personal life remained complex. On returning to school as a married woman, she found that she was still attracted to Steve, and he to her. Yet she believed that she could keep her marriage vows and still work side-by-side with Steve. Their relationship included a foundation of true friendship and political committment.

Besides, Mamphela was busy. In 1970, she chaired the local South African Students' Organization committee. As chair, she spoke out in public and ran meetings. She also organized discussion sessions to educate students about SASO, and she worked on membership drives. In addition, she chaired the annual national SASO conference at Natal Medical School. She had become a political leader.

Mamphela was also involved in SASO's attempts to reach the black community outside of the university by opening a health clinic for the poor. Along with other university medical students, Mamphela treated patients at the clinic. But as important as the health care she provided was her message of self-esteem and pride: Black Consciousness.

Mamphela found herself becoming "increasingly self-confident and vocal in student meetings and in national student forums," she recalls. In fact, she was becoming "quite an aggressive debater." She was a surprise to men who didn't expect aggressive debate from women. Many were intimidated by her. Soon her women friends, too, were speaking out at the meetings. Though they were not yet talking about women's rights, they were insisting on being taken seriously. They made themselves part of the dialog and took on leadership roles.

Mamphela and others also joined non-university protests. Off campus, South Africans were protesting Nelson Mandela's imprisonment. He and other African National Congress leaders had been behind bars for more than seven years; other activists were being imprisoned at an alarming rate. The stories leaking out of the prisons were more frightening than ever—stories of torture and police brutality. Between 1963 and 1969, according to journalist Donald Woods, at least twenty people had died mysteriously while in the hands of police. The deaths were listed as suicides or accidents—slips in the shower, falls down stairs—but most people believed that the police had killed them.

By this time the apartheid government had outlawed political protests. Funerals, however, were still allowed. So students and others staged huge funeral services for those dying in police custody. These often turned into rallies, protests, and even riots. Shouts of "*Amandla! Awetha!*"—"Power! To Us!"—were accompanied by the African salute to black power: a clenched fist with raised thumb.

These prisoners are chained in the courtyard of Robben Island Prison, the jail where Nelson Mandela was imprisoned. At this notorious maximum security facility, located on an island offshore from Cape Town, Mandela organized political education for his fellow prinsoners.

The government's response to the uprisings across South Africa and to the student activism on South African university campuses was more repression. More squatter camps were bulldozed; more people were sent off to the homelands; more people arrested.

Mamphela continued to work on her political activities at school. Her marriage, though, was failing. As early as December 1970, she knew it was in trouble. Her husband had quit school and turned to alcohol; what's more, whenever they were together, they fought.

In June 1971, Mamphela served as chair of the annual SASO conference at Natal Medical School. She did well in this responsible position and felt successful and hopeful when she joined her husband afterward for vacation. But she found her home in shambles. Her husband had turned the house into a *shebeen* (informal saloon). There, he drank all day with the township's "no-hopers," Mamphela recalled. As soon as she walked in the door, she and her hus-

What are townships, homelands, and squatter camps?

The apartheid government wanted to control where black South Africans lived, so that black famlies would not live in white neighborhoods. The government created two systems for black residences—townships and homelands. Townships were built outside cities and near industrial areas. Black South Africans who worked in these areas were expected to live in the townships. These were crowded and short of housing, conditions that the government fostered to discourage people from living there. What's more, to live in townships, people had to have their passbooks stamped, proving they were employed nearby. Often men were forced to live alone in dormitory-style hostels; their families were not allowed to stay with them.

Homelands were tracts of land in rural, usually extremely poor areas given to black South Africans to live on, somewhat like the American system of reservations for Native Americans. Black South Africans were assigned to a homeland and forbidden to live anywhere else unless they had legal permission stamped in their passbooks. Large numbers of families were deported from the cities and forced to live in homelands, often splitting up families.

As a result of these systems, squatter camps developed around cities, where people threw up shacks out of scrap building materials and stayed illegally, to be close to jobs or their families. Conditions for those living in the camps were terrible, with no electricity or sewage systems. The government raided the camps, arresting and deporting people without passbooks, and when that didn't reduce the camps, they bulldozed thousands of homes without warning. The stress of living in such a place was tremendous—a woman might come home from a long day of work to find her house flattened, her belongings gone, and her children sent to an unkown place.

band began to fight. Mamphela decided this would be the last fight in this marriage. She left Dick.

Mamphela was now free—but Steve Biko was not. He had fallen in love with Ntsiki Mashalaba, and had married her. What's more, he would soon be a father. He had also become the national leader of student activism. His own studies had suffered in the process, and he was no longer in school. He was focusing entirely on building Black Consciousness.

Along with social worker Bennie Khoapa, Barney Pityana, Mapetla Mohapi, Mamphela, and other leaders, Steve Biko established the Black Community Programmes (BCP). Through this new organization, the activists set up self-help programs in black communities. Before long, they were creating a new publication, the *Black Review*, to spread the Black Consciousness message.

In December 1971 Mamphela led a student work camp at Winterveld, a huge squatter camp near Pretoria, and saw some of South Africa's worst urban poverty firsthand. Her goal at Winterveld, in addition to offering medical help, was to explain Black Consciousness to the people, and encourage their self-confidence. But she quickly became discouraged. She saw the utter powerlessness that the poor felt. Pass laws kept them constantly on the run from police, because few of them had legally updated passes. Police raided their neighborhoods in the middle of the night, chasing them down as they ran out back doors and jumped out windows. Anyone slow enough to get caught was arrested and fined for pass law violations. They could not get jobs because they didn't have passes, and they could not get passes because they were there illegally.

People living in squatter camps had little hope left, and no dreams. For many, simple survival had become the goal for each day. Seeing such destitution made Mamphela realize how deeply apartheid reached into people's lives. It truly had made them feel inferior. Black Consciousness and black pride were even more greatly needed than she had imagined.

Police tear down the make-shift homes in squatter camps, attempting to stop black South Africans from living in areas not specifically authorized.

While Mamphela was in Winterveld, Steve Biko was launching the Black People's Convention, to help organize the growing number of Black Consciousness groups across the country. This was an important step for Black Consciousness because it established a network; now, activists could be more coordinated, could hold more conferences to discuss their plans and ideas, and could broadcast their message more fully.

Mamphela and Steve, back from their separate assignments, worked closely together on this exciting new network, sharing their many hopes for a free future. Happy to be together, they also admitted that they felt as in love as always. They told themselves that they could have a secret relationship without hurting Steve's wife, Ntsiki. Mamphela writes that she told herself that even though a partial commitment was not what she wanted, this was the best that she could have under the circumstances, and it would have to be enough.

Mamphela's school classes took up less and less of her time. Finally she had arrived at her last year at medical school. She had changed and matured quite a bit from the politically naive girl who had allowed a professor to pin a National Party button on her blouse. She found it difficult to overlook the racism of some of her professors.

One medical professor, in particular, irritated her. He was condescending to his students, referred to black male patients as "the old boy" or "old John," and included apartheid politics in his lectures. Mamphela stopped attending his classes and was summoned to his office. She arrived ready to stand her ground. She told him that she would return to his classes only when and if he stopped talking politics. He threatened to report her defiance; she said, "do what you will." The professor was shocked. It was unheard of for a black student, especially a woman, to defy the authority of a white professor. Once again, Mamphela was blazing her own trail. "As a woman, an African woman at that, one had to be outrageous to be heard, let alone be taken seriously," she explained years later. Women were easily made invisible in male-centered cultures, including South Africa's. Mamphela would not be treated as invisible.

Mamphela graduated from medical school and moved on to an internship at a hospital in Durban, and to more political work. By this time, SASO, with Mamphela in its inner circle, had expanded enormously. Its leaders oversaw self-help projects and medical clinics. They held leadership training seminars for members on college campuses throughout South Africa. Their newsletter circulated Black Consciousness ideas throughout the country.

In 1972, SASO also organized strikes on university campuses. Thousands of students took part, and upwards of 600 students were arrested. The organization had become famous for its activism. Black Consciousness was taking hold, too. Mamphela would hear the idea of black pride surfacing in speeches and in rallies. People were listening, and many black South Africans no longer felt inferior to whites. They were declaring that they were not just "nonwhite," they were black, human, and had a powerful history of their own in the lands of South Africa.

The apartheid government was not pleased. In 1973, it took action, banning eight SASO leaders. The police scattered the leadership to isolate them from one another. Barney Pityana was banned to a township in Port Elizabeth. Steve Biko was banned to King Williamstown.

Steve, however, refused to be isolated. He opened an office that quickly became the center for the community of activists. Mamphela commuted from Durban to see Steve on weekends, keeping up both

Soweto, a township ten miles southwest of Johannesberg, was the scene of the 1976 anti-Afrikaans student protests. After troops violently suppressed the demonstration, more than 600 people were left dead.

What does it mean to be banned?

Banning was a uniquely South African punishment. When the government could not legally put individuals in prison but wanted them out of the way, it banned them. Banned people, the law said, could not speak out in public, could not be quoted, could not write for publication, and could not meet with more than one person at a time. They could also be confined to certain areas. Since it was illegal for banned people to speak in public, write, or be quoted, their ideas could not reach the public. They therefore could not influence people. They became invisible—or so the police hoped.

her personal relationship with him and her work for Black Consciousness.

Meanwhile, the security police harassed the entire Biko family and circle of friends. They swooped in and searched homes, recorded the names and addresses of anyone who dared visit Steve, tapped the phones, monitored the mail, and kept Steve under constant surveillance. This was not unusual; this was how the police treated most banned South Africans. It was, however, annoying and often frightening.

Mamphela transferred to a hospital nearby, and she and Steve grew closer than ever. She soon realized that she was pregnant. Later, during the last months of this difficult pregnancy, she went to her mother's house in the Transvaal. There, in 1974, she gave birth to a baby girl, whom she named Lerato, a Sotho word meaning "love." She left Lerato with her mother while she returned to King Williamstown to find a new job and set up a household. But before she could get back to pick up her daughter, the baby very suddenly died of pneumonia.

Mamphela, heartbroken, followed Lerato's tiny casket to its final resting place alone; Steve was not

Crowds of people celebrated the opening of the Zanempilo Community Health Centre. Improving healthcare for black South Africans has been a long struggle for many activists.

allowed to attend his daughter's funeral because of his banning orders. Mamphela dealt with the loss with unflagging courage, and by forcing herself to work even harder than ever. She believed that her baby would not have died if the kind of proper medical facilities she was fighting for had been available to rural black communities like hers.

The banning of Steve Biko had made international news. And far from silencing him, the banning had earned him even greater fame than before. National and international journalists sought him out in King Williamstown to discuss Black Consciousness.

Mamphela continued to be central to the group's work. Soon she was heading up the most ambitious project yet for the Black Community Programmes: the Zanempilo Community Health Centre at King Williamstown. Mamphela organized the clinic from the ground up. She ordered supplies, hired nurses, and supervised the entire operation. Finally, in 1975, she opened its doors to patients.

The clinic itself was a tremendous boon to the people of the region. Most black South Africans had to travel for hours to a hospital that would accept them. Then they would wait in line for hours more before a doctor saw them. Often the doctor would give them a quick glance, dismiss them within five minutes, and almost always would treat them as inferiors. At Zanempilo, the patients would be treated with dignity—respectfully and professionally. They would receive the best medical care Mamphela could give them. What's more, her staff would educate them about health practices.

The clinic was also a chance for black South Africans to prove "what their own people could do," explained Mamphela's friend, Father Aelred Stubbs, in his memoir. The clinic was run *by* black South Africans *for* black South Africans, and the medical care was top-notch. As it turned out, the clinic also raised the consciousness of both patients and staff, but not through political discussion. It inspired people because it was an example demonstrating what blacks could accomplish. "The *spirit* of Zanempilo . . . proclaimed the gospel of Black Consciousness far more effectively than any 'political talk' could have done," wrote Father Stubbs. Zanempilo reflected Mamphela's ideals; it was dynamic, dignified, and responsible.

For Mamphela, this was a time of hard work, high hopes, and joyous gatherings. In addition to directing the clinic, she also began managing Black Community Programmes in the Eastern Cape. She was at the hub of the movement, surrounded by excitement, and busy every day with work toward South Africa's liberation. She had truly hit her stride. She

Dr. Ramphele served as the head doctor at Zanempilo until she was banned. Respect for patients was an important message of the health center.

was a confident, professional doctor and activist. And, although the workload was often overwhelming, she was seeing the rewards of her work. And she imagined that she could sense hope in the air.

During this period, Mamphela made a famous visit to the editorial offices of liberal white South African journalist Donald Woods. Like many white South Africans, Woods did not understand Black Consciousness. He thought that because it separated blacks into their own all-black organization, it played into the hands of apartheid, which wanted blacks and whites separated. Mamphela visited Donald Woods to urge him to learn about Black Consciousness by speaking personally with Steve.

Donald Woods was accustomed to the humble attitude that black South Africans assumed in front of whites. But Mamphela walked through the door with confidence—the kind of confidence usually shown by white men in South Africa. She spoke intelligently and directly. She drew up a chair, explained Black Consciousness, and convinced Donald Woods to see Steve.

This was an important achievement, because Donald Woods soon became a vocal supporter of the Black Consciousness movement. His positive editorials on Black Consciousness educated thousands of white South Africans about the new black philosophy and the conditions blacks were living under. (He, too, would eventually be banned. But he would escape with his family out of South Africa, and publish a book, *Biko*, that would help reveal the truth about South Africa to the entire world. It would also be made into a movie, *Cry Freedom*.)

By 1976, many black South Africans had absorbed Black Consciousness values and were developing a sense of personal and black pride. As they were overcoming the feelings of inferiority that the apartheid system had taught them, they were also growing frustrated. They were poor; they were hungry; their schools were shabby. Laws restricted them from getting good jobs and even prevented them from living together as families. And new, more restrictive laws were passed every year. They could see no hope for a better life. There came a time when people began to see that they had nothing to lose. Therefore, they were willing to risk all. They were ready to fight to the death. The apartheid government, however, did not understand that there had been a shift, and that the country was ready to explode.

The government issued an order that black South African students would be taught in Afrikaans—the hated language of the apartheid government. Most black South Africans used English as their nonnative language. Students in Soweto, a crowded

Students protest against being taught in Afrikaans. Limiting education was one way in which the apartheid government maintained racial segregation.

township outside of Johannesburg, protested. Thousands joined in a protest march, singing, chanting, and jogging down the main streets of Soweto. Soon the streets were full of high school and elementary school students. "Away with Afrikaans" was the message they had for the South African government.

The police blocked the street with trucks, tanks, and men in riot gear. They set dogs loose on the children and fired tear gas into the crowd. Then they fired bullets into the crowds of children, killing ten-year-old Hecter Peterson on the spot. But instead of running off and huddling in fear, the children did the unexpected. They regrouped and turned on the police in rage. And it was a rage that the police had never seen before.

The children, joined by adult residents of Soweto, became a huge, angry group. They threw stones, smashed windows, overturned cars, and set trucks and houses on fire. They attacked government buildings, set fire to beer halls and bottle stores. And they attacked the security police themselves, who fought them with clubs and guns.

The protesters paid dearly. At least 600 died. And the Soweto riots spawned riots throughout the rest of the year and into the next year. Police arrested thousands, but the people kept protesting, and also holding stay-at-homes and school boycotts. The people were in open rebellion against the government.

Police in King Williamstown blamed much of this on Steve, Mamphela, and the Black Consciousness movement. They detained Black Consciousness leader Mapetla Mohapi, and a few days later reported that he had committed suicide. As a doctor, Mamphela attended an examination of the body and could clearly see that her friend had not committed suicide. He had been killed in his cell by the police.

Mamphela herself was detained the next month, in August of 1976. She was imprisoned for almost five months, sharing her cell with other women, some of whom she knew as fellow activists. During this time, Steve was also jailed for a few months. All over South Africa, women and men were being tossed into jail, many beaten, some tortured, so Mamphela knew she was luckier than many. Though she was in jail, she and the other women were unharmed. What's more, she wrote, they "naively imagined" that the open rebellion in the streets meant that the end of apartheid was just "around the corner." Mamphela put her time to use by studying and taking exams in a correspondence course for a Bachelor of Commerce degree. She also had time to examine her life.

When she was released from prison on December 28, Mamphela sat down to talk with Steve. He had had time to think, too. Neither of them was content with their relationship. Steve, Mamphela recalls, vowed that he was going to start divorce proceedings. He was ready "to follow his heartfelt desire to share his life with me as his marriage partner," she wrote in her autobiography. Mamphela was ecstatic. Soon they would be together always. As she set back to work at the clinic, her "heart danced for joy."

Over the next few months, she and Steve spent every day together. They hardly noticed the increasing hostility of Captain Schoeman, the security police officer assigned to make sure Steve did not disobey his banning orders.

Women protested in support of other women activists, like Mamphela, who were detained in prison. The sign listed the names of women in Pretoria Central jail, and the number of years they had been imprisoned.

Chapter 6

BANNED BUT NOT SILENCED

The day the security police came for Mamphela, she was taken by surprise. She had just walked into Steve Biko's office when Captain Schoeman charged through the door, barking that Mamphela must come with him immediately.

When Mamphela refused, Schoeman grabbed her and began to drag her out the door. Steve stepped in, demanding that Schoeman let Mamphela go. But the Captain had the upper hand here. He called in extra security police. They dragged Mamphela out the door and tossed her into the back of a police van.

The van careened and swerved this way and that as it sped to the police station with Mamphela, unable to get a handhold, lurching back and forth inside it. Then it screeched to a halt and police hauled her out of the van and into the station.

She was banned! She immediately protested. She could not accept that it was correct. She had responsibilities at the clinic, a family, and patients to look after. The police could not just drag her away. Captain Schoeman and his police sat smugly listening. They knew that they could just drag her away—and they did.

The trip north was a long, dark, cold drive along back roads through the eastern part of the country. The police took the back roads as an extra precaution, Mamphela figured, to make sure no one who knew her saw where she was going. Her feeling of isolation increased as she watched the dark land-scape pass by. Tzaneen! Of all places, they had found one that she had never even heard of.

After a two-day ride, Mamphela was left in Tzaneen with five rand in her purse and knowing no one. She needed help, and she guessed she might get it from a church. She arrived on the church doorstep, and when they heard her story, nuns and priests, both black and white, rushed to take care of her—and to get her to a phone. Steve spread the news to her family and friends, who were relieved to know that she was all right.

Mamphela was not one to surrender without a fight. She quickly found a way to return home, though only temporarily. She fearlessly seized on a small error in the banning documents: her name was spelled wrong. She could argue that the police had grabbed the wrong woman!

She sped back home to a joyous reunion with her Zanempilo staff, friends, and Steve. The journalist Donald Woods, who by now was a good friend and a regular visitor at Zanempilo, described the reunion in his book *Biko*. "I remember admiring Mamphela's steely nerve," he wrote, "and Steve's. . . . Neither gave any indication of tension, although both must have known that informers would have tipped off the security police about her return to the clinic, and that a raid might occur at any time." Of course, the raid did occur, but not until Mamphela had had ten days at Zanempilo, time to say farewell to friends and Steve, and to turn the clinic over to her replacement.

When she was returned to the Tzaneen district, she knew that she was there to stay. She moved into a house in Lenyenye Township. It was a poor, depressing little village, yet when Father Stubbs visited Mamphela during her first month there, he reported that she "was in high spirits and already spreading the gospel of Black Consciousness." If the authorities had hoped to discourage Mamphela from her goal of raising the consciousness of black South Africans, they were to be sorely disappointed. If she couldn't run Zanempilo, she would work on transforming Tzaneen.

The people in the small village were kind. One sent a teen-aged girl, Makgatla Mangena, to stay with Mamphela both as company and housekeeper. Mamphela's mother visited too, and Mamphela phoned Steve frequently to stay in touch with friends back home. She discovered very soon that she was pregnant—how glad she was that she had taken a chance and had a reunion with Steve.

She was to see Steve one more time, and was able to give him the good news about her pregnancy in person, when she was summoned to King Williamstown to testify at his trial for minor apartheid violations. Then, back at Lenyenye, Mamphela settled in for what she knew would be a long stay. With the financial help of the Black Community Programmes, which, though outlawed, was still functioning, she opened a medical clinic for Tzaneen.

Mamphela's pregnancy interrupted the project. Pregnancy was never easy for her, and this one required strict bedrest. In a coincidence that Mamphela always considered eerie, even somewhat mystical, the threatened miscarriage came at the same time as Steve Biko's final imprisonment and torture.

On August 18, 1977, Steve was stopped at a roadblock and arrested for traveling outside his banning

Steve Biko's death in 1977 was a crisis to thousands to whom he was a hero and a source of hope for an end to apartheid. A crowd at his funeral mourn, while one woman holds his picture and a wreath.

area. Over the next several days, he was interrogated by security police, who blamed him for the riots and protests that were still raging since the Soweto uprising. The police, sometimes in groups of five, beat Steve with fists and pipes until they had beaten him into a coma. He never woke from the coma, and died on September 12, 1977, of massive head wounds.

The police claimed at first that Steve had died from a hunger strike, then that he had died accidentally in a scuffle with the police. Apartheid government leaders at first made jokes about Steve's death, but then, on seeing the international and public outcry, backtracked and tried to appear sympathetic.

Mamphela would not find out the details of Steve's death for many years to come. But she knew, and so did most of South Africa and soon the world, that the police had beaten him to death. Steve's funeral was a massive event held at the King Williamstown stadium. Oxen drew the coffin toward the cemetery until pallbearers lifted it and held it shoulder high— "an impulsive gesture which was to become the hallmark of funerals of comrades to come," wrote Lindy

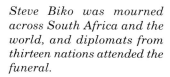

Steve Biko was mourned across South Africa and the world, and diplomats from thirteen nations attended the funeral.

Wilson, a friend and South African educator. Donald Woods reported that 20,000 black South Africans and several hundred white South Africans attended the funeral. Many more were stopped at roadblocks and prevented from attending.

Mamphela, isolated and hospitalized to protect her pregnancy, could not attend the funeral. Steve Biko's wife, Ntsiki Biko, attended the mass funeral, along with her two sons. For Mamphela, however, these were lonely, tormented days. "It was not just the end of the vibrant life of a gifted person with a sense of destiny," she wrote, "but it was the death of a dream." The dream was both personal and national in scope. The dream was Black Consciousness and a proud hope for a better future in South Africa.

A month after Steve's murder, on October 19, 1977, all Black Consciousness organizations were outlawed. The Zanempilo Centre was taken over by the government. Donald Woods and several colleagues were banned, along with other activists and friends of Mamphela. Many more throughout the country were detained in jails.

Mamphela's son, Hlumelo, which means "the shoot that grew from a dead tree trunk," was born on January 19, 1978. Mamphela, exhausted by the struggle of giving birth, but "so grateful" to have her son beside her, was also mourning the loss of Steve. He would remain her greatest love. But she reminded herself that she was not the only woman suffering in the struggles against apartheid.

Women were losing husbands, sons, daughters, sisters, mothers and fathers. Women were being tortured with beatings, with electric shocks, and worse, and many were dying. Many black South Africans were starving, living in shacks, and being chased out of their beds in the middle of the night. At least Mamphela would be able to support and feed her family. At least she could raise her son. And she could help others who were victims of the repressive system. What's more, as she looked at the generosity and poverty of the people around her, she says, she was "filled with humility. . . . I had to stop feeling sorry for myself and get up and walk."

Mamphela planted a garden with vegetables, flowers, and fruit trees. She created a home. Now when she stood at the front door, she was greeted with the sweet scent of blossoming roses. Her young son had a house to grow up in and a yard to play in. She returned to work at the clinic she had begun before Steve's death.

Over the next year, Mamphela built up her clinic and expanded her influence in the district. The government's reaction was to reduce the area to which she was confined. Now she had to stay within the

How did South African women organize to end apartheid?

Women participated in the protests, including demonstrations, stay-at-homes, and boycotts. Many also founded organizations to resist apartheid; most of these organizations were eventually banned. Many of the women were themselves banned, others were imprisoned. Some went into exile. A few of the major women's organizations were:

The Federation of South African Women (FSAW), a mother (umbrella) group that served black South African women, Indian women's organizations, Coloured women's organizations, white women from the Congress of Democrats, as well as trade union women.

The African National Congress Women's League led the 1955 march against pass laws of 20,000 women in Pretoria. In the 1990s, it convinced the African National Congress to include women's concerns in the new constitution; it also supported female ANC candidates for political office.

The Black Sash, formed by white women, and named for the black mourning sashes the women wore, held protests and also advised and aided people arrested for pass law violations.

The United Women's Organizations, which later became the United Women's Congress, helped women both politically and economically. In squatter camps, the organization set up facilities for clean water. In townships, it organized child care for women workers. It also held workshops to raise the women's consciousness.

township of Lenyenye. Nevertheless, her clinic, the Ithuseng Community Health Programme, continued to grow. And Mamphela continued to find ways to bring her message of empowerment to the people. Before long, she had a van to transport supplies and to get her team to the many villages scattered through nearly one hundred square miles of the district. Her outreach programs were teaching women modern hygiene in caring for their children. And she had won the approval of the village chiefs. They were

A woman of the Xhosa people from northern South Africa carries her child on her back. There are many different ethnic groups in South Africa, who maintain their traditional cultures in different ways. In the nineteenth century, the Xhosa people put up some of the strongest resistance to European settlers.

defying the government by encouraging villagers to participate in Mamphela's programs.

Mamphela soon expanded her clinic further, until in 1981 it was a complete center, the Ithuseng Community Health Centre. Archbishop Desmond Tutu, an active South African religious and political leader, came to celebrate the expansion. He had helped Mamphela find funding for the center. Many other friends joined her that day, too—friends from her Zanempilo days, along with influential friends from inside and outside South Africa. For a banned person who was supposed to disappear from public life and become invisible, Mamphela was having a great deal of influence and a great number of distinguished visitors!

What's more, Mamphela was empowering the women around her to believe in themselves. She did it with knowledge. In addition to teaching women about modern health techniques, her center orga-

Mamphela takes a break from her work at Ithuseng health clinic with some of the people of Tickeyline Village, near Lenyenye, the village where she lived for eight years.

nized self-help projects for them. One was the production of small mud stoves that reduced the need for firewood. Since women were responsible for gathering wood, these stoves freed them to do other things. She also began a daycare program and an adult literacy program. She encouraged self-reliance and self-confidence—fundamental Black Consciousness ideals. In addition, she returned to her correspondence studies, earning degrees in Tropical Hygiene and Public Health, and completing her Bachelor of Commerce degree.

Over the years, she continued to be visited by friends and political allies. Helen Suzman, one of the few progressive members of parliament during apartheid and one who supported racial equality throughout her political career, visited Mamphela. Bruce Haigh, from the Australian Embassy, stopped in. Old friends from Mamphela's student days at the University of the North visited frequently, too. It was through the university friends that she met the man who would become her second husband, Sipo Magele.

Sipo Magele was both handsome and educated. He lectured in pharmacy, a subject Mamphela shared an interest in. He seemed to be a good choice in a husband, and Mamphela wanted a companion. She became pregnant, and this was the most difficult pregnancy of all. Her son was born prematurely at eight months, and was so small at birth that the doctor gave up on him. A nursing sister rescued him and nursed him along until Mamphela could tend to him.

Mamphela's new son, Malusi, born on March 16, 1983, arrived into a South Africa that was undergoing change. Protests were ongoing. The security police response was angry and violent. And the list of people who had died while in custody was still growing; it now included its first white South African, Neil Aggett. Individuals were targeted outside of prison, too. Ruth First, a brave activist and the wife of activist Joe Slovo, was murdered by a letter bomb in 1982.

By this time, even many white South Africans were calling for change. Though most did not want to

In parts of South Africa with few services such as electricity or running water, women may spend up to four hours daily collecting water from wells. Collecting firewood can also be time-consuming, and is a job often done by women.

lose their advantages—the peaceful white neighborhoods, preference for jobs, and an excellent educational system—they also did not like all the negative press about their country. South Africa was expelled from the United Nations for human rights violations in 1974. Their sports teams were no longer welcome in international events. And the sanctions that the world was placing on their businesses was costing them money. Many were calling on their government to put an end to the chaos and violence.

Prime Minister P. W. Botha began to talk about "moderate reform." He had a new slogan: "Adapt or Die." He repealed a few apartheid laws. Black South Africans could once again legally form unions, and all jobs were now theoretically open to black workers.

It was clear that change was in the air. Finally! As Mamphela looked back six years to when Steve was still alive, when they had all "naively imagined" that liberation was just around the corner, she had to smile at her own innocence. One could just now begin to sniff the scent of some future freedom, but it was still well off in the distance. Getting around this corner to liberation was proving to be a long, long hike for all of them.

Mamphela's banning orders expired in 1983, and she was once again "free" in a nation that did not grant her any true freedoms at all.

Chapter 7
LEADING THROUGH SCHOLARSHIP

Mamphela stayed in Lenyenye for a year after her ban was up and then moved to Port Elizabeth, a coastal town on the southeastern tip of South Africa. Finally, she was returning to city life. What's more, she would also be with her husband again. She and Sipo Magele had been living apart because Magele's work had taken him to Port Elizabeth while Mamphela's had kept her in Lenyenye.

Once in Port Elizabeth, Mamphela found herself facing daily irritations. Though her job as a medical officer at a large hospital was as demanding as Sipo's job, he still expected her to come home from work every day and cook his meals, clean the house, take care of the children, do the shopping, and also do all the other chores that it takes to run a household.

Mamphela was exhausted. She found herself caught between two worlds. In one world, she was rewarded both intellectually and financially. She was an equal and working alongside colleagues at the hospital, learning new techniques and gaining new scientific knowledge.

In the other world, she was failing and could never meet her husband's traditional demands. "Being black, woman, mother, and professional places one in a challenging position anywhere in the world, but more particularly so in South Africa," Mamphela explained. Although women's lives had changed greatly, men's expectations of women had changed very little. Of course, Mamphela had hoped that Sipo would have the courage to be different. It would have taken courage for him to face his friends and declare that he and his wife would live equally, side by side, because his friends would surely have ridiculed him. But Sipo was not different.

The final straw came one evening, Mamphela recalls, after she had spent a hard day at the hospital and was facing a long evening of domestic chores. In a scene that could have happened in many parts of the world, a tired Mamphela cooked dinner while her husband dozed in a chair. Beside him, Malusi, then eighteen months old, was crying. Sipo ignored him and continued to rest contentedly. Mamphela could not accept such thoughtless behavior. She knew at that moment that her marriage was over.

Like women all over the world, South African women have been seeking greater equality. They've

After they left Lenyenye, Mamphela and her two young sons, Hlumelo, age six, and Malusi, age one, lived in Port Elizabeth and Cape Town, and life became very different.

started numerous organizations to focus on specific problems. Mamphela herself, though, had always worked for the greater cause of black South Africans; in fact, she realized, she had not challenged men through the years when they had refused to do their share of domestic chores. And the chores were important because they symbolize all the other male privileges that also went unchallenged.

Mamphela was thinking more and more about the different kinds of injustice people face. In South Africa, blacks faced discrimination based on their race. Many women of all races dealt with inequality, even in their own homes, simply because they were women. Black South African women experienced a double dose of injustice.

Within two months of her decision to leave Sipo, Mamphela found a job in Cape Town working with Francis Wilson, a longtime colleague and a professor of economics at the University of Cape Town. Then, despite Sipo's objections and anger, she packed up and moved down the coast to Cape Town.

She leased a house for herself and her sons in Guguletu, a township reserved for blacks. Mamphela's house was a nice three bedroom, but it did not protect her or her children from the violence that shook all of the townships during the 1980s. Guguletu was a dangerous place. It had the highest per capita murder rate in the world, Mamphela reports. Criminal violence by *tsotsis* (criminal gangsters) was so rampant that it frightened most township people off the streets and into their homes before dark.

The violence was a by-product of apartheid. In Guguletu there were streets where people crowded into shacks, often with one hundred women, men, and children living in a space suited to a single family. The shacks were made of "zincs" (corrugated tin), toilets were outhouses, and water was fetched from a faucet that could be as much as half a mile away. In the winter it was freezing; in the summer wretchedly hot. But even worse than the conditions was the lack of hope. What could the future offer to people whose education was poor (on purpose), who were limited by law to low-level jobs, whose every move was controlled by the government through the pass system? The future offered no hope; the present offered nothing but poverty, hunger, and despair. The results of these conditions were crime and violence.

Mamphela quickly discovered for herself that the school system was overcrowded and almost non-functional. Although he was still in elementary school in 1985, Hlumelo was frequently sent home by teachers who were concerned about their students' safety. Schools were also often closed for entire days or weeks by boycotts and stay-at-homes.

Meanwhile, Prime Minister P. W. Botha's plan for moderate reform was lurching on. In 1983 he had pushed for a constitutional change that gave limited voting rights to "Coloured" and Asian citizens—but not to black South Africans. All real political power stayed in the hands of the whites, so nothing was really changing. The plan angered most "Coloured" and Asian South Africans, who saw that the apartheid government was trying to trick them. It enraged black South Africans. The black population saw the plan as an attempt to fool the world into thinking that real changes were being made in South Africa. And they weren't.

The Western Cape is known for its diverse environments, with stunning mountain views, lush bays, desert plains, and Cape Town at its center. On either side of the cape are the Atlantic and Indian oceans.

White South Africans, on the other hand, saw the reforms "as major concessions," according to Alistair Sparks, a well-known South Africa journalist. They saw themselves as generously holding out an offering, and being rejected out of hand. They had promised to institute some small changes, and they did not understand that what blacks wanted was the power to change their *own* lives. They did not see that their new plan kept white South Africans still in the role of "fathers," with everyone else still being cast as the "children." As long as the "fathers" held onto control, the "children" could never grow up—they would never be treated with the same respect as white adults.

Unrest in the townships escalated, and the apartheid government's response was almost always the same: tear gas and gunfire. Mamphela's house, she soon discovered, was located right on the funeral procession route. Since many political protests and riots began with mass funeral gatherings, Mamphela often found herself in the middle of the battles. Hlumelo quickly learned to recognize the warning signs of danger: the security police warning, the sound of tear gas landing in the street, the people screaming and running, the guns firing, the whishing-slamming of *sjamboks* (police whips) as protesters were chased.

Little Malusi was too young to figure out what was really dangerous and what was just everyday violence. He ran and dove under his bed every time gunfire sounded anywhere within earshot. He became an anxious, nervous, and frightened child, Mamphela reports.

Mamphela herself was living a dual life, part of it in the violence, noise, and dust of Guguletu and the other in the quiet peace of the suburbs, at the University. "It is amazing how successful the apartheid cities have been in separating the lives and problems of black township residents from those of whites in the suburbs," she commented. As she looked at the contrast between her own home and the homes of white South Africans, she added, "It was hard to believe that one was living in the same city." White South Africans, partly because of this separation, were still fooling themselves into believing news reports that told them that apartheid was working well, and that black South Africans were happy and satisfied with their lot.

People outside of South Africa, where the news was uncensored, were less easy to fool. In 1984, Archbishop Desmond Tutu won the Nobel Peace Prize because of his humanitarian efforts for the people and against the evils of apartheid.

Black South Africans continued to fight the apartheid government. In the mid-1980s, workers held more strikes than ever before—more than 390 strikes by 240,000 workers by the end of 1985. The violence grew, with attacks on the homes of black policemen, town councilors, and anyone seen as aiding the apartheid enemy. Government buildings were burned and police stations were bombed. In 1984, 174 people died during the violence; in 1985, the number of dead reached 879.

Under Botha's leadership, parliament repealed a few more small apartheid laws, including the laws against interracial marriage. Botha, who under a new constitution had become president, was still trying to show a better face to the world. But black South Africans were still not fooled. They continued to demonstrate and protest. The government imposed a state of emergency.

Mamphela, meanwhile, came under heavy criticism. Some activist friends, pointing to the tremendous disruptions in the country, questioned her safe life at the peaceful university. Was she giving up the struggle? Had she sold out? Shouldn't she be on the front lines organizing marches and protests? Mamphela grappled with these questions and, though the criticism stung, she knew that she was doing important work.

In partnership with Francis Wilson, she researched and wrote a book that presented new ideas to the public. She reported on how violence was affecting South Africa's children. Some were being beaten, permanently injured, or killed. Others were becoming violent themselves, and even criminal, as they were caught up in the chaos around them. She and

Archbishop Desmond Tutu leads the Truth and Reconciliation Commission in 1996 in Cape Town. Here he works with some of the sixteen members of the Commission. They hope for openness and justice to heal enough of the nation's sorrow and anger to make possible forgiveness, and a united, reconciled society.

Wilson suggested that political movements took advantage of children. Adult leaders, afraid to face police bullets and tear gas, sent children into the streets in their place. They hoped that the police would not fire on the children, but they knew that the police often did. Children were killed. No one on either side of the struggle liked seeing themselves in this light.

Mamphela also faced the violence in the township along with every other resident. One day, for example, a young man running from the security police raced into her house and hid in the bedroom while Mamphela and her sons were having lunch. The police stormed in on the heels of the man, and after barging through the house and searching all the rooms, found him and dragged him off. The young man later charged that Mamphela had betrayed him.

This was a life-threatening claim. For such betrayals, people were routinely executed in the townships by protestors who believed that even violence against other black people was justified in the struggle against apartheid. Mamphela fearlessly stood up to the man and several witnesses supported her innocence. She and her sons were safe, for the time being.

One day in 1986, the violence finally overwhelmed even Mamphela. Her housekeeper, Nomvume Sotomela, called to tell her that protesters were on their way to set fire to the community center next door. Mamphela leaped into her car and drove straight home through the chaos of the emerging protest. She gathered up Nomvume and the children and raced off. She moved into a university staff house until she could purchase her own home.

She now had the salary to buy a house, but the law made it illegal for her, a black person, to buy property in the white suburb of Mowbray, where she wanted to live. So like many other black South Africans at the time, she bought her house under a "front" name; in her case, the university allowed her to register the house in its name.

The United States had been lukewarm in imposing sanctions against South Africa for its apartheid system. In 1986, however, the U.S. Congress overrode a veto by President Reagan to impose sanctions. Sympathetic protests began in the United States. On some college campuses, students built and moved into symbolic squatter camps. International banks, in this same period, refused to extend their loans to South Africa. South Africa was feeling the financial and political pressure of the world. But P. W. Botha could not find a way out of the nation's violent cycle,

Behind the city of Cape Town is beautiful Table Mountain. The city is one of South Africa's main harbors and the legislative capitol.

and he was not yet willing to completely give up the apartheid system. He was in the position that many had warned him of: he was doing too little too late. Botha's ministers, meanwhile, with his approval, began to hold secret meetings with Nelson Mandela, who was still in prison.

In the midst of all of this, in 1988 Mamphela was invited to the United States on the Carnegie Distinguished International Fellowship. She happily accepted, and she and her sons spent the 1988–89 school year in Boston, Massachusetts. She worked at the Bunting Institute at Radcliffe College, and the children attended school. The Bunting Institute provides women scholars with funding and support for research. She suddenly found herself in what for her was a paradise.

Living outside apartheid South Africa for the first time, she and her sons flourished. The boys freely visited museums, went to movies, and made friends.

What challenges face South Africa today?

South Africa still faces serious problems. Violence did not end with the end of apartheid. It still runs in the streets, with armed robberies, carjackings, assaults, and murders as daily occurrences. Many have asked why. The answer is complex. But it includes anger, frustration, and disappointment. Many blacks see little change for themselves personally since they elected a president for the first time in 1994. Poverty amongst black South Africans is still deep and widespread, and the gap between the rich and the poor is wide. Job opportunities are opening to blacks, but slowly. Also, the result of the Bantu Education Act is still being felt. It left the nation's educational system in shambles, and much of South Africa's population ill-prepared to compete in the modern world. The new government has a great deal of work to do to repair the damage done by apartheid.

Mamphela loved the opportunities for learning provided by her new environment. "Such luxury I had never known before," she says. "I sat back and immersed myself in the community of women scholars and the wealth of Harvard University's library resources." She had long, in-depth discussions with powerful women—poets, painters, sculptors, astrophysicists, mathematicians, political scientists, anthropologists, and more. "It was an intellectual feast," she wrote.

While Mamphela worked in the United States, South Africa went through a turbulent year, with widespread strikes, school boycotts, and mass protests. Still, the apartheid government was not ready to give in. In 1988, it banned the United Democratic Front, a group of activist organizations, along with the members of thirty other organizations against apartheid.

When Mamphela returned to South Africa in 1989, she returned to a country in the throes of violent change. Many things were happening simultaneously. Prisoners were staging hunger strikes. Meanwhile, still unbeknownst to most South Africans, Nelson Mandela was deep into negotiations with the white South African government for an end to the struggle. Both sides wanted to see peace.

Mamphela visited Nelson Mandela during his last years in prison. She and Mandela agreed on many issues, but not all. The traditional leadership of South Africa's indigenous ethnic groups was one area of disagreement. Mandela accepted these systems. Mamphela pointed out that they were undemocratic, based purely on inherited positions, and sexist in the extreme. Male dominance was a foundation of the sys-

How did South Africa's struggle against apartheid compare to the Civil Rights Movement in the United States?

In fundamental ways, the struggle to end apartheid in South Africa was similar to the Civil Rights Movement in the United States. In both struggles, people sought equality from their governments, school systems, and workplaces. In both instances, too, people sought basic human dignity and fairness in their societies. Both began with peaceful demonstrations and appeals to the humanity of the people in power. Both also escalated into confrontations with police and arrests of demonstrators.

The two nations, however, have different histories, cultures, and populations and these factors undoubtedly created two different responses to civil rights demands. The United States was eventually embarrassed by its unfair laws and, at the urging of leaders such as the Reverend Martin Luther King Jr., repealed the laws and sought integration. South Africa, however, reacted by passing more and more restrictive laws. White South Africans are the minority population, and they desperately sought to continue their dominance over all South Africa—its economy, politics, and society. Their determination to maintain apartheid cost the nation dearly in lives lost, money wasted, and resources squandered.

tem. As Mamphela explained her position, "Mandela's face darkened," Mamphela later wrote. She knew she had ruffled the great man, but she did not back down. She knew it was important for Mandela to think deeply about equality for women. He was the leader of black South Africans and would soon be the nation's leader. Her words would stay with him.

Mandela's efforts at negotiating a peaceful settlement to South Africa's violent struggle paid off toward the end of 1989. Walter Sisulu and the other activists who had been sentenced to life in prison with Mandela in 1964 were released from prison. Mandela was freed a few months later.

The stage was set for the end of apartheid.

Chapter 8
SHAPING A NEW DEMOCRACY

Euphoria swept South Africa. Apartheid was over!

Exiles were returning home. Thousands had fled over the decades to Europe or the United States to escape certain arrest, or even death. Now many were rejoining families they had not seen in twenty years. Families within South Africa who had been separated by apartheid's laws were also reuniting. A new South Africa would soon be born.

The focus shifted from defeating the old apartheid government to creating a new one. The word on all tongues was *transformation*. The country would be transformed, or changed, into a democracy of all races. For the first time in its history, South Africa would be a free country for all of its people. It would take hard, careful work to build a government in which everyone in this diverse country was represented and *felt* represented, and to repair all the damage done by apartheid.

The criticism that Mamphela had endured when she joined the University of Cape Town (UCT) died away as fellow activists realized the importance of her work. The education of black South Africans had been inferior under the Bantu Education Act; rebuilding the schools would be a priority with the new government. Black South Africans appreciated having a black woman in a position of power and influence at a prestigious university. Mamphela could open doors to Black students. Though blacks were 76 percent of the population, they were just ten percent of the student body at UCT.

It didn't help that almost all of the faculty was white and male. In fact, UCT was a fortress of white male power. White males ran the university, chose who would be admitted to the university, and taught almost all of the classes. What's more, UCT ceremonies, from freshman orientation to graduation, were copies of white European university ceremonies: African tones and rituals were nowhere to be seen. Mamphela was in a position to change that, and she was intelligent enough, strong enough, and forceful enough to do it, too: she would prove this over the next few years.

Mamphela was becoming known outside of South Africa, as well. Her work took her to far-ranging points on the globe. In 1990, she served on a panel of South African leaders gathered to educate American lawmakers on the complexities of South Africa. While there, Mamphela brought up women's equality, facing down one fellow South African panelist who told her she sounded like a "scratched record"—an accusation frequently used to silence women who speak up on behalf of women. Mamphela continued to speak up, nevertheless.

South Africa was experiencing the first thrills of integration. "Whites Only" signs were torn down from beaches, parks, public toilets, movie houses, restaurants, and other public places. All people were free to travel and live wherever they chose, and all races had an equal right to buy, sell, and own property anywhere in the country. New regulations also helped some 300,000 black householders to obtain ownership of the houses they lived in. And the government repealed the hated Population Registration Act of 1950: this meant no more passbooks! Police could never again stop a black citizen in the street and imprison her just for not having her passbook stamped.

The new South Africa faced tremendous challenges. A different kind of violence shook the nation. Now disputes broke out in some homelands, as well as between black political groups, most notably between the Inkatha Freedom Party and the African National Congress. Some of this was secretly provoked by white government officials to divide black leadership. Some reflected age-old political battles. Some was the result of simple greed and criminal activity. None of it, however, could stop the transformation of South Africa from going forward.

By the end of 1991, a convention to discuss transformation and a new South African government had begun. It was called the Convention for a Democratic South Africa (CODESA). Mamphela, that same year, had moved into a position of more influence. Through her books and work, she had established herself as a top social anthropologist, and was awarded a Ph.D. in social anthropology from UCT. She was also appointed deputy vice chancellor of UCT. Now second only to the vice-chancellor, she was a leader of the university. She was one of the few blacks with such power and prestige in all of South Africa.

The first half of the 1990s were times of both success and tragedy for Mamphela. In 1991, her niece Morongwa died at Baragwanath Hospital during a routine operation after a miscarriage. Though legal segregation of hospitals was over, black patients still often received low-quality care in hospitals that had

Dr. Ramphele, being sworn in as vice-chancellor, was congratulated by President Nelson Mandela. As activists against apartheid Mamphela had been banned for six years and Nelson Mandela was imprisoned for twenty-seven.

been poorly supplied and staffed for so long. Mamphela would never know if her niece's death was due to negligence. Then in 1993, her brother Sethiba, with whom she had baby-sat their younger brother Poshiwa back in 1953, died of cancer.

As she had often done when faced with personal tragedy, Mamphela focused on her work. Her duties at the university kept her long hours, and she was invited more and more often to national conferences and on international tours. She was on the boards of several companies. She chaired the Independent Development Trust, which raised funds for scholarships and educational projects. Her goal was to help wealthy industries learn to open opportunities to poorer communities. She also furthered her work as a writer, with three books about black South Africans published in the early 1990s.

In 1993, as the country continued to move toward its first all-citizen election, Nelson Mandela and for-

What was the Truth and Reconcilation Commission?

South Africa's history of imprisonment, torture, and murder of protesters left the country with a great deal of unresolved anger. In response, at the end of apartheid, South African leaders formed the Truth and Reconciliation Commission (TRC). Chaired by Archbishop Desmond Tutu, the commission held trials of those accused of violent, political crimes that took place during the struggles. The commission could recommend amnesty for those who came forward and completely confessed their crimes, but only if the crimes were committed for political reasons and not for criminal, personal gain. The security police who killed Steve Biko applied for amnesty in 1997. Their trial revealed the horrifying details of his last hours. Many other, similar stories surfaced.

mer South African president Frederik de Klerk won the Nobel Peace Prize for their efforts to transform South Africa. In 1994, Mandela was elected president of the new government of South Africa. In his opening remarks to parliament that May, he reminded the nation that "freedom cannot be achieved unless women have been emancipated from all forms of oppression." Mamphela was pleased.

In 1995, the Truth and Reconciliation Commission, headed by Bishop Desmond Tutu, began its investigation into crimes committed during the apartheid era. Five security police eventually came forward to describe Biko's last days and the torture that killed him. They appealed for amnesty from the Truth and Reconciliation Commission. Their appeal was denied.

The same year, Mamphela became vice-chancellor of the University of Cape Town, the equivalent of university president in the United States. This was a first for black women in South Africa. She immediately set a new tone for the university. It would no

Mamphela with her son Hlumelo at his graduation from the University of Cape Town in 1998. Dr. Ramphele balanced her work as vice-chancellor, an anthropologist, and an activist with raising two strong sons.

longer be an all-white university with European rituals. It would be South African.

Academic leaders from the United States, England, and around the world, as well as President Nelson Mandela, attended Mamphela's inauguration ceremony. Mamphela Aletta Ramphele, dressed in official university robes, smiled proudly at the distinguished leaders gathered before her. Meanwhile, beside her on stage, her mother performed a praise-song. As her mother strode up and down the stage, Mamphela says, she "was telling me I come from a great stalk and I have to succeed but I have to remember where I come from." Her mother's praise-singing, like Mamphela's grandmother's from childhood, was in Sotho. Speaking Sotho in a public ceremony was another first for UCT! Mamphela was happy—she had brought her heritage with her on stage.

Mamphela promised to make changes. When she took over in 1996, ninety percent of the professors were white males. Her job as she saw it was to transform the university into a place that reflected and served all of South Africa. The "central issue" of the decade centered around "the need for *regstellende aksie* . . . to put right that which went wrong in the past," Mamphela explained in her university's student newspaper. She encouraged black South Africans and women to apply for faculty positions. She wanted to create a faculty that included people of all races, both women and men.

Mamphela also reached out to black students, so that by 1998, blacks made up 50 percent of the student body, a rise from 10 percent in 1988. Mamphela did not neglect girls, either. To reach out to them, she urged her engineering, math, and computer science professors to meet with schoolgirls and to encourage them in these fields. She also started the African Gender Institute in 1996. Based at the University of Cape Town, it is in some ways like the Black Consciousness programs of the 1970s. It both studies the problems of inequality and finds ways to make changes. The institute's goal is to give women access to positions of power in education, government, and business.

Mamphela works long days at the university, meeting with her deputy vice-chancellor, directors, and others who oversee UCT operations for her. She is frequently called on to make speeches, both as guest of honor and as host, at national and international gatherings. And she continues to be a mother to her two sons, both of whom have grown into fine young men. They are "the most wonderful sons," she reports. "Not only because they love me so much, but

What is the new South Africa doing to effect change?

When Nelson Mandela took office in 1994, he faced a monumental task. The entire country of South Africa outside of the white sections needed to be built or rebuilt. School buildings needed to be constructed, textbooks purchased, and teachers trained or hired. Segregated hospitals needed total rehabilitation. Police departments needed training, and all facilities needed integration.

In addition, most black areas had little or no running water or electricity. Mandela's government set about to make as many changes as the budget would allow. His officials reported that every day between 1994 and 1998, electricity was added to 1,300 homes, clean water brought to 1,700 more people, and 750 telephones installed. But still, in 1999 almost two-thirds of black South Africans had no modern plumbing, more than half had no electricity, and 89 percent had no telephones. Nearly all white South Africans already had these modern conveniences.

Dr. Ramphele enjoys working with today's young South Africans even before they get to the University of Cape Town. She is helping students develop their leadership skills early.

because they are brutally frank with me and they keep me on the straight and narrow."

Leaders in all walks of life—business and science, as well as education—have been called on to contribute their talents to redesigning life in South Africa. "Every day one participates in the re-making and shaping of the new democracy," says Mamphela. She contributes to the new South Africa through her leadership at the University of Cape Town. There, she is turning her hopes into reality. "My vision of UCT," she said in 1996, "is that of a powerhouse of intellectual energy on the tip of Africa."

Mamphela's empowering ideas have undoubtedly reached, through her speeches and leadership, into the community and into government circles. In 1999, as Nelson Mandela stepped down from the presidency, his political party, the African National Congress, supported numerous women running for office. In his last official address to the South African Parliament, Mandela expressed his hope that "we can and shall build the country of our dreams." In June 1999, thousands of voters of all races went to the polls, democratically choosing Mandela's deputy, Thabo Mbeki, as the second president of a free South Africa.

In 2000, Mamphela plans to go to work for the World Bank as a director for health, education, and social protection. She told the *Chronicle of Higher Education* that she sees this as an important opportunity for a South African women "to put on [the bank's] agenda issues that are of importance to those of us living in the developing world."

Mamphela's work in the Black Consciousness movement is rewarded today as young black South Africans find their way to self-confidence and embrace Black Consciousness ideas as their own. She has come a long, long way from her childhood in apartheid South Africa, from the day when the dominee of her village told her that a young black woman becoming a doctor was a pipe dream. She made it past many "gatekeepers" along the way who tried to fence black students, and especially girls, out of white schools. Today, as vice-chancellor of a top South African university, she has become a gatekeeper herself. But as she sees her job, it is not to keep the gates closed, but to keep opening them again and again until opportunity is open wide to all.

CHRONOLOGY

1947   Mamphela Aletta Ramphele is born on
            December 28.

1948   Apartheid begins when the National Party wins
            the elections.

1952–60   The Defiance Campaign led by the African
            National Congress protests apartheid; the
            Freedom Charter is endorsed by activists
            against apartheid; 20,000 women protest pass
            laws; and police open fire on demonstrators in
            1960 in what becomes known as the Sharpeville
            massacre.

1962–67   Mamphela attends boarding schools, then begins
            pre-med studies at the University of the North;
            in May 1967, her father dies.

1968–70   Mamphela transfers to the University of Natal
            and meets student activists, including Black
            Consciousness leader Steve Biko. Mamphela
            becomes a leader in the South African Students'
            Organization and Black Consciousness. She
            marries Dick Mmabane.

1971–72   Mamphela graduates with medical degree and
            works on Black Consciousness projects. She
            divorces Dick Mmabane.

1973   Steve Biko is banned to King Williamstown and
            sets up headquarters there.

1974   A daughter, Lerato Biko, is born and dies in
            infancy.

1975   Mamphela leads the Black Consciousness team
            opening the Zanempilo Community Health Centre

	at King Williamstown. She also manages Black Community Programmes in the Eastern Cape.
1976	Students in Soweto riot when told they are to be taught in Afrikaans, and many are killed by police. Mamphela is imprisoned for five months, then banned to Tzaneen.
1977	Steve Biko is murdered in prison, September 17.
1978	A son, Hlumelo Biko, is born. Mamphela opens clinic in Tzaneen, which soon grows to become the Ithuseng Community Health Centre.
1981–83	Mamphela earns degrees in tropical hygiene and public health. She marries Sipo Magele.
1983	A second son, Malusi Magele, is born. Mamphela's ban is lifted.
1984	Mamphela divorces Sipo Magele. She begins work at the University of Cape Town, and lives in Guguletu Township.
1986–87	Mamphela buys a house in Mowbray. Her book on children and violence is published. She wins the Carnegie Distinguised International Fellowship.
1988–89	Mamphela spends the 1988/89 academic year at Radcliffe College. Back in South Africa, she visits Nelson Mandela in prison and discusses with him women's roles and women's rights.
1990	Mandela is released from prison; this marks the beginning of the end of apartheid.
1991	Mamphela becomes deputy vice-chancellor of the University of Cape Town and earns Ph.D. in social anthropology from UCT.
1994	Free elections are held in South Africa. Nelson Mandela is elected president.
1995	Mamphela's autobiography is published in South Africa. She is chosen as the University of Cape Town's vice-chancellor.

1996   Mamphela's autobiography is published in the United States as *Across Boundaries: The Journey of a South African Woman Leader*.

1997   Steve Biko's killers appear before the Truth and Reconciliation Commission.

1999   President Nelson Mandela steps down, and the second free elections are held in South Africa. Mamphela works on a book on youth in post-apartheid South Africa, and leads the University of Cape Town toward integration.

GLOSSARY

Afrikaans Language descended from the language of the early Dutch immigrants to South Africa.

Afrikaners People descended from the early Dutch immigrants, often mixed with French, German, and other European ancestry.

Amandla Power. A word used by South Africans opposed to apartheid, often with a raised fist to emphasize the point.

Amnesty Official pardon for political crimes.

Apartheid An Afrikaans word literally meaning "apartness"; the political system supported by a series of segregationist laws held in effect by the National Party in South Africa from 1948 to 1990; abolished in 1993.

Banning Forced someone to stay in an assigned area. In South Africa, banning was a government punishment like house arrest.

Bantu Refers to the family of languages of southern Africa, but was used during apartheid to mean people of African descent, as a derogatory word.

Boycott To refuse to buy a product or participate in an activity in hopes that this refusal will encourage change. South Africans boycotted buses, schools, and businesses at various times.

Detainees People held in custody; in South Africa, people jailed under special laws allowing arrests without evidence or trial.

Exiles People who fled the country to escape persecution, prison, or execution for their political views.

Sanctions Actions taken as a way of discouraging or punishing a country, such as boycotts of trade with South Africa.

Segregation A government or community policy of separating people according to racial or ethnic heritage.

Social anthropology The study of communities and cultural systems.

Stay-at-homes General strikes, with workers in a variety of jobs staying home.

Transformation A word used in South Africa to refer to post-apartheid changes and the creation of a new society based on equality of opportunity.

Acronyms

ANC African National Congress

ANCWL African National Congress Women's League

BCP Black Community Programmes

CODESA Convention for a Democratic South Africa

NUSAS National Union of South African Students

PAC Pan Africanist Congress

SASO South African Students' Organization

SRC Students Representative Council

TRC Truth and Reconciliation Commission

UCT University of Cape Town

UDF United Democratic Front

UN United Nations

UWCO United Women's Congress

FURTHER READING

Books About Mamphela Ramphele and South Africa

Denenberg, Barry. *Nelson Mandela: No Easy Walk to Freedom*. New York: Scholastic Trade, 1991.

Lazar, Carol. *Women of South Africa: Their Fight for Freedom*. Boston: Little, Brown, 1993. (Introduction by Nadine Gordimer, photos by Peter Magubane)

Mandela, Nelson. *A Long Walk to Freedom*, abridged version, edited by Marc Suttner and Coco Cachalia. Boston: Little, Brown, 1995.

McKee, Tim. *No More Strangers Now: Young Voices From a New South Africa*. NY: DK Ink, 1998.

Pratt, Paula Bryant. *The End of Apartheid in South Africa*. Lucent Overview Series. San Diego: Lucent Books, 1995.

Ramphele, Mamphela. *Across Boundaries: The Journey of a South African Woman Leader*. NY: The Feminist Press, 1997.

Smith, Chris. *Conflict in Southern Africa*. New York: Simon & Schuster, 1993.

Internet Sites

South African Wildlife Parks
(http://www.africam.com)

African National Congress
(http://www.anc.org.za)

South African Bookstore
(http://www.bookchat.co.za)

The Daily Mail and Guardian Newspaper
(http://www.mg.co.za/mg)

University of Cape Town
(http://www.uct.ac.za)

INDEX

Page numbers in *italics* indicate illustrations

Acknowledgements

This book could not have been completed without the help of several people along the way. First and foremost is Mamphela Ramphele herself. She has supplied us all with great insights into her thoughts and into South Africa's struggles through her autobiography, *Across Boundaries*. Then, in addition, she took time out from an incredibly busy and productive schedule to give me additional information. Thanks are also due to the University of Cape Town, the staff of Dr. Ramphele's office, and Ceri Oliver-Evans for help with photographs. My thanks also go to Goodie Tshabalala Mogadime for valuable background on life in South Africa, and to Peter Midgley for research assistance. In addition, I am grateful to Kay Driscoll, the librarian and research expert, who helped find some of the more obscure sources for this book. And, finally, on a personal level, I wish to thank Terry Tintorri and Jameson Mah for their unwavering support through this project and always.

Picture Credits

About the Author

Judith Harlan, a journalist and author of books for young adults, places her focus on women's issues. She is the author of *Girl Talk: Staying Strong, Feeling Good, Sticking Together*, a book of confident thoughts for young girls, and *Feminism: A Reference Handbook*. Her book, *Sounding the Alarm: A Biography of Rachel Carson* received high praise, and she was honored with the Carter G. Woodson Outstanding Merit Award from the National Council of Social Studies for *Hispanic Voters: Gaining a Voice in American Politics*. Harlan holds an M.A. from San Fransisco State University and has been an observer of feminist activities and goals since the 1970s.